Allegra felt the silent magnetic pull of his dark brown gaze, her breath stalling somewhere in the middle of her chest as their eyes locked. The silence was so thick she felt as if it was going to choke her. Her heart began to thump a little irregularly as his gaze slipped to her mouth for a nanosecond, before returning to her wide green eyes.

'Fine…' he said again, running a hand through the thickness of his hair in a manner that appeared to Allegra to be slightly agitated. 'I'll…er…let you get back to work.'

She watched as he turned and walked with long, purposeful strides up the length of the corridor before disappearing from sight through the swing doors at the end. She blew out a little uneven breath and gave herself a mental shake. *Don't even think about it*, she told herself sternly.

TOP-NOTCH DOCS

He's not just the boss, he's the best there is!

These heroes aren't just doctors,
they're life-savers.

These heroes aren't just surgeons,
they're skilled masters. Their talent and
reputation are admired by all.

These heroes are devoted to their patients.
They'll hold the littlest babies in their arms,
and melt the hearts of all who see.

These heroes aren't just
medical professionals.
They're the men of your dreams.

He's not just the boss, he's the best there is

IN HER BOSS'S SPECIAL CARE

BY
MELANIE MILBURNE

First published in Great Britain 2006
Large Print edition 2007
Harlequin Mills & Boon Limited,
Eton House, 18-24 Paradise Road,
Richmond, Surrey TW9 1SR

© Melanie Milburne 2006

ISBN-13: 978 0 263 19554 5

Set in Times Roman 15¾ on 18½ pt.
17-0707-59399

Printed and bound in Great Britain
by Antony Rowe Ltd, Chippenham, Wiltshire

Melanie Milburne says: 'I am married to a surgeon, Steve, and have two gorgeous sons, Paul and Phil. I live in Hobart, Tasmania, where I enjoy an active life as a long-distance runner and a nationally ranked top ten Master's swimmer. I also have a Master's Degree in Education, but my children totally turned me off the idea of teaching! When not running or swimming I write, and when I'm not doing all of the above I'm reading. And if someone could invent a way for me to read during a four-kilometre swim I'd be even happier!'

Recent titles by the same author:

Medical Romance™
A DOCTOR BEYOND COMPARE
  Top-Notch Docs
A SURGEON WORTH WAITING FOR
  24:7
HER PROTECTOR IN ER

> **Did you know that Melanie also writes
> for Modern Romance™? Her stories have
> her trademark drama and passion, with the
> added promise of sexy Mediterranean heroes
> and all the glamour of Modern Romance™!**

Modern Romance™
THE VIRGIN'S PRICE
THE SECRET BABY BARGAIN
BOUGHT FOR THE MARRIAGE BED
BACK IN HER HUSBAND'S BED

To my nephews and niece Ben, Tommy, Peter and Katherine (Kathy) McNamara. You have all been through so much in your young lives and I am in awe of how you have coped. I love each of you very dearly and dedicate this book to you in acknowledgment of your struggles, your tragedies and your joys that I will always share with you, not with a glance of pity but with the steady gaze of compassion.

I would also like to give my heartfelt thanks and appreciation to the doctors and nursing staff of the Royal Hobart Hospital's Intensive Care Unit for their invaluable help in the research conducted for this novel as well as Dee Nally from Salamanca Pharmacy for her advice. Thank you all!

CHAPTER ONE

'WHAT do you mean, he wants me to stop my research on the coma recovery assessment project?' Allegra Tallis asked the nursing sister on duty in Intensive Care. 'That's outrageous. The CEO gave me his full support, I've got ethics approval and I've got funding!'

Louise Banning gave her a sympathetic look. 'I know all that but Dr Addison is the new Director of ICTU and A and E now, and what he says goes.'

'Not if I can help it,' Allegra growled. 'I'm not giving up months of research to satisfy some control freak's demands to run a tight ship. Who does he think he is anyway? He might be the new director but if he thinks he can tell me what to—'

'Dr Tallis?' A deep male voice spoke from just behind her. 'We haven't had the opportunity to meet since I arrived. I'd like to speak to you in my office—now, if you don't mind.'

Allegra swung around to see a tall dark-haired man in his early thirties towering over her, the deep brown intensity of his eyes as they connected with hers making her throat move up and down involuntarily in a tiny swallow.

'Oh…Dr Addison. Well, I'm just seeing a patient right now…' she said.

His gaze hardened as one dark brow lifted in an arc of derision. 'Sister Banning is your patient, is she?'

Allegra tightened her mouth. 'No, of course not—I mean in the unit. I can see you in about five minutes.'

'Make if four,' he said. 'I've got a crammed schedule this morning.' He continued on this way, his starched white coat brushing against her arm as he went past.

Louise's brows rose expressively once he was out of their hearing. 'Not the best first meeting, I would say.'

'No.' Allegra frowned crossly. 'Well, I've been on night shift for the last week. I wasn't here for his welcome thingy.' She twisted her mouth and added, 'God, what a pompous idiot.'

'Yes, but a rather good-looking idiot, don't you think?'

She gave a little snort. 'If you have a thing for the tall, dark, brooding type.'

'You never know—he might improve on acquaintance,' Louise said. 'He's got a very good reputation. He's been head-hunted especially for the post so he can't be all that difficult to work with.'

'Yeah, well, I still think Dougal Brenton should have got the job,' Allegra said. 'He's been at Melbourne Memorial for years, and instead they bring in someone just because he's worked overseas in a war zone.'

Louise glanced at her watch. 'Could be this will be a war zone if you don't keep your appointment with him,' she said. 'I'll keep on eye on things here. You'd better go.'

'Thanks, I won't be long.'

Dr Joel Addison's office was in the middle of the multi-million-dollar newly built intensive care and trauma unit, providing the city of Melbourne with a state-of-the-art trauma and acute care centre—in fact, the largest in the country. With twenty-six ICU beds, a burns unit, a ten-bed trauma receiving area and two fully equipped operating rooms all in the same complex, it offered a breadth of care in one site that was second to none.

Allegra gave the director's door a quick hard knock and waited for the command to come in. When he gave it in a blunt one-word response, she opened the door to find him seated behind his desk with a large pile of paperwork spread out before him.

He rose as she came in, his height seeming all the more intimidating in the confines of his office.

He offered her a hand across his desk. 'We haven't met formally. I'm Joel Addison, the new director of ICTU and A and E.'

Allegra placed her hand in his briefly, her eyes skittering away from the chocolate-brown depths of his. 'Allegra Tallis.'

'Please, sit down, Dr Tallis,' he said. He waited until she was seated before resuming his own seat, his dark eyes steady on hers. 'You're an anaesthetist, I believe.'

'Yes. I'm on a twelve-month rotation in ICTU,' she answered, trying not to fidget like a naughty schoolgirl called into the headmaster's office. Her mouth felt suddenly dry and she would have loved to run her tongue over her lips to moisten them, but didn't dare do so with those dark, fathomless eyes seemingly watching her every movement.

A heavy silence pulsed for a moment or two. Allegra felt each thrumming second of it, wondering what he was thinking behind the screen of his darkly handsome features.

She hadn't had time to reapply her lipstick and her hair was falling from its clip at the back of her head. Heaven knew what her eyes looked like after a week of night duty. She'd barely been able to see out of them that morning when she'd dragged herself out of bed, but she knew there were shadows on top of shadows beneath them that no amount of cover-up could have concealed.

Her brief meeting with him in the corridor hadn't given her time to examine his face in any detail but now she could see how lean and chiselled his cleanly shaven jaw was. His skin was tanned, as if he spent outdoors whatever time he had away from the hospital. His hair was thick and dark with a hint of a wave running through it, and the way it was currently styled it looked as if his long fingers had been its most recent combing tool. His eyes were a deep brown, so dark she couldn't tell what size his pupils were as they seemed to be indistinguishable from his irises.

'I've heard some interesting things about you, Dr Tallis,' he said into the silence.

'Oh?'

He leaned back in his seat, his posture positively reeking of indolent superiority as his eyes held hers. 'Yes.'

She held his unwavering gaze with steely determination, not even allowing herself to blink. 'And?'

'I have some concerns about your research project. I find it hard to justify. I would appreciate your explanation of its scientific merit. As far as I can see, it would be more appropriate at a mind and body expo than in an ICU unit.'

Allegra straightened her spine, her green eyes flashing with fury at his condescending attitude. 'I've had full ethics approval for my coma recovery assessment project,' she informed him. 'And I have a research grant from the hospital.'

'The ethics is not what I take issue with, Dr Tallis, it's the scientific merit, unfortunately, in my opinion, spelt out by the first letters of the project name. As far as I can see, the research committee seemed swayed by factors other than scientific validity.'

She shifted in her seat again. 'I don't exactly know what you're getting at, but if you read the proposal…' It hit her then, the acronym he had made of her project. CRAP. She inwardly seethed but she was loath to allow him the credit of making a joke out of something she took very seriously.

His cool little smile already suggested to her his inbuilt cynicism. She'd seen scepticism before, but somehow Dr Joel Addison took it to a whole new level. She silently fumed at his attitude, wishing yet again that Dougal Brenton had been given the job of new director.

'I have read it—several times. How long have you been at Melbourne Memorial?' he said.

'I did my training here,' she answered.

'So you haven't worked anywhere else?'

It was amazing how someone who had worked overseas always had to hold it over the heads of those who hadn't, Allegra thought resentfully. She'd seen it time and time again. Even registrars, who, after a short stint in the UK or even in a developing country, came back with a superior attitude, as if Australia was a backwater wasteland with limited training experiences.

'No,' she said with more than a hint of sarcasm. 'I haven't as yet had that wonderful privilege.'

He ignored her comment to ask, 'What is the gist of this project—in one sentence?'

Allegra forced her shoulders to relax, wanting to come across as coolly efficient and in control. 'I'm examining the effect on coma recovery of different methods of sensory contact, using a BIS monitor as a key detector of effect,' she said.

'Sensory contact…' He lifted one dark brow in query. 'Such as?'

She gave him a very direct look, mentally preparing herself for his reaction, a reaction she had seen far too many times to hope that this time would be any different. 'Reiki therapy, massage therapy, music therapy and aromatherapy.'

'So…' The leather of his chair creaked as he leaned back even further, his expression unmistakably mocking. 'It sounds to me that if ever I'm feeling a little tense in the shoulders, I should head right on down to ICTU, feign a coma in one of the incredibly expensive beds and hope for a quick massage from you. Is that right, Dr Tallis?'

Allegra felt her anger rising to an almost intolerable level. 'I believe that human touch is an important part of a patient's recovery, comatose or not,' she said through tight lips.

'Important—I doubt it,' he returned. 'What ICU specialises in is ensuring good oxygenation and blood pressure maintenance—if brain injury is not too severe, recovery will occur. As far as I can see, these alternative therapies are marginal at best, maybe counter-productive at worst. There is no scientific evidence that they are effective, and attempts to prove their unlikely effectiveness are unaffordable in this unit.'

'That's not true. Reiki therapy has been shown to increase local circulation and—'

'Dr Tallis.' The little mocking smile was still in place. 'Increasing the circulation by touching someone's arm is not the same as increasing cerebral blood flow. And these smells and so-called natural aromas, your oils or whatever—what if someone suffers an allergic reaction to them?'

'I've done a literature review on—'

'I've seen the "literature review", as you call it, hardly peer-reviewed journals—more like the latest women's magazines.'

'That's so totally unfair!'

'Look, Dr Tallis, you've spent—what is it now?—six years at medical school and a further four years studying anaesthesia. It's called medical science. That's what we practise here, and it's damn expensive. Leave the quackery to the quacks and let's get on with the job of saving lives. That is what you have been trained to do and that is your primary responsibility while you are working in ICTU.'

'Patrick Naylor, the CEO, has given me his approval,' she put in with a tilt of her chin.

He held her defiant gaze for an infinitesimal pause, before asking, 'Is it true that you and he are an item?'

Allegra felt hot colour rush up into her face. How

had he found out about her one dinner with
Patrick? How had *anyone* found out about it? One
date did not constitute a relationship as far as she
was concerned and, besides, Patrick was still
getting over a nasty separation. She had agreed to
have dinner with him more because she had felt
sorry for him than any degree of attraction on her
part. It had been her first date in eighteen months
and certainly no one's business but her own.

'I hardly see that my private life is any concern
of yours,' she said with a heated glare.

'No, indeed, but if it interferes with how ICTU
is run then it becomes of great concern to me. I'm
here to put ICTU at Melbourne Memorial on the
map as best practice for trauma reception and
acutely ill patients, and I will not tolerate either my
reputation or that of this hospital with the introduction of alternative "medicine" practices that do not
have a scientific leg to stand on. We've a got a big
enough workload with conventional medical care.'

Allegra got stiffly to her feet. 'The work I'm
doing on my project does not interfere with my
regular workload. I do most of it in my spare time.'

He rose to his feet, his superior height immediately casting a shadow over her. 'I'm going to
give you a month to get whatever results you can,

but then I'm reviewing it. And let me tell you, if there are any complaints about the methods you are using then I'll pull the plug on your study there and then. This is a new unit and every professional and political eye is focused on it to make sure the hefty amount of public money that's been allocated to it has been spent wisely. And my reputation is riding on it as well. I don't want the press to get wind of trauma patients having their tarot cards read as part of their recovery program in ICTU.'

Allegra had never felt so incensed in her life. Her hands were clenched by her sides so she didn't give in to the temptation to slap that supercilious smirk off his face. She didn't trust herself to speak even if she could have located her voice; it seemed to be trapped somewhere in the middle of her throat where a choking nut of anger was firmly lodged.

'Good day, Dr Tallis,' he said, moving past his desk to open the door for her. 'I'm sure you've got patients to see. I don't want to keep you from them any longer.'

She strode past him with her head high, her mouth tight and her eyes sparking with ire.

'Oh, and one more thing,' he said, just as she'd brushed past.

She stopped and turned around to face him, her expression visibly taut with rage. 'Yes?'

His eyes twinkled with something that looked suspiciously like amusement as he took in her flushed features. 'If you don't mind me saying so, for someone who is so into alternative relaxation therapies, you seem a little tense. Have you thought about booking in for a massage yourself?'

'Why?' she asked with a curl of her lip. 'Are you offering your services?'

He suddenly smiled, revealing perfectly even white teeth. 'I'm not sure in this case that my touch would have the desired effect.'

'Not unless I was completely comatose,' she clipped back, and stalked out.

CHAPTER TWO

'How did your meeting with the director go?' Louise asked later that morning.

'Grr…'Allegra answered with a fiery look. 'Every time I think of that man I want to punch something.'

'That doesn't sound like you,' Louise remarked. 'You're always the one telling the rest of us how to chill out and relax. Is he really going to put a stop to your study?'

'He's giving me a month to prove that it's worthy of "medical science"—his version of science anyway,' Allegra answered. 'But how can I do anything in a month? It all depends on what patients come in. We haven't had a coma patient since poor Alice Greeson, three weeks ago, and she didn't recover.' She blew out a sigh of frustration. 'I have to change his mind. I really want to do this study, Louise—it's important to me.'

The hospital intercom suddenly blared out in a tinny voice, 'Code Blue, Surgical Ward,' repeating it several times.

'Got to go, Louise,' Allegra said, heading for the lift. 'I'm on the crash team this morning.'

The surgical ward was on the sixth floor, but when Allegra got to the bank of lifts none of them seemed to be moving. She shifted from foot to foot impatiently, before turning and heading for the fire exit. She started running up the stairs two at a time, glad she'd resumed her fitness programme now that Christmas had passed.

When she arrived on the ward the curtains were drawn around one of the beds in room two, the crash trolley, two nurses and the intern already doing cardiac massage on the patient.

'What's the story?' she asked, as she pushed aside the curtains.

'Sixty-five-year-old male, two days post right hemicolectomy,' the intern answered. 'The nurses were getting him out of bed for a wash and he collapsed. Looks like a PE, maybe an infarct.'

'Is the floor anaesthetist on the way?' Allegra asked.

'He might not be coming,' one of the nurses answered. 'There's some sort of complicated case going on in Theatre that's tied up a lot of staff.'

'I'll intubate him,' Allegra said, moving to the head of the bed and picking up the sucker from the emergency trolley. 'You'll need to help me,' she said to the nurse on her left.

'But I'm just out of grad school,' the young and rather nervous-looking nurse said. 'I'm not sure what I'm doing. I've never been to an arrest before.'

'Just do what I say, you'll be fine. Turn on wall suction,' she said, as she suctioned the patient's mouth and reapplied the oxygen mask. Allegra picked an endotracheal tube and checked the laryngoscope battery. 'OK,' she said to the intern who was bagging the patient between cardiac compressions from the surgical ward nurse, 'I'll tube now. Put on cricoid pressure, will you?'

The intern stepped aside and applied cricoid pressure while Allegra removed the mask from the bag and oxygen. She rapidly intubated the patient and connected the oxygen, handing the bag back to the intern to continue ventilation while she secured the tube. The medical registrar, Peter Newton, had by now arrived and was looking at the ECG trace.

'He's got a rhythm,' he said. 'Looks like VT. We'll need to cardiovert. I'll do it.' He took the paddles from the defibrillator and dialled up 100, applied the paddles to the patient's chest and called,

'Clear.' All staff removed their hands from the patient while the intern continued to ventilate. With a jerk the patient's back arched and then fell back as the current was applied.

'He's in sinus rhythm,' Allegra noted, looking at the monitor. 'What drugs do you want up?' she asked the registrar.

'He's had an infarct is my guess. There's a few VEBs. I'll start a lignocaine infusion, but we need to get him round to ICTU and keep him well oxygenated. I'll contact my boss and bring him round to ICTU for a consult.'

'You look as if you could do with a bit of oxygen yourself,' Allegra said, taking in Peter's flushed features. 'Are you OK?'

He gave her sheepish look. 'The lifts were busy. I had to run up two flights of stairs. I guess I'm not as fit as I thought.'

'Lucky you,' she said as she moved aside for the trolley men who had come to do the transfer. 'I had to run up six.' She gave him a smile and added, 'Go and have a glass of water. I'm going back to ICTU anyway so I'll hand the patient over.'

Allegra accompanied the patient, Gareth Fisher, to ICTU and had not long informed the surgeon, Bruce Crickton, of his patient's condition when the ICTU registrar Danielle Capper approached.

'Dr Tallis, can you help me on bed five?' she asked. 'It's Mr Munsfield, the Whipple procedure. He was extubated yesterday and was doing OK, but his sats have gone down in the last hour and he's on 60 per cent oxygen. He's become febrile and has abdo pain.'

'Sure.' Allegra began walking with Danielle to the far end of ICTU, where bed five was situated. 'Have you had any bloods done?'

'They should be on the fax now in the office. I'll grab them and see you there,' Danielle said.

Allegra reached bed five and after greeting Fiona Clark, the nurse in charge of beds four and five, took a look at the patient, who was pale, slightly cyanosed and very breathless. His sats monitor showed 80 per cent, BP 100 and pulse 110.

'Deep breaths, Mr Munsfield,' Fiona instructed the patient. 'I've just given you some IV morphine for the pain.'

'What was the last temperature, Fiona?' Allegra asked.

'Thirty-nine. It's been up all morning,' Fiona answered.

'Where's the pain, Mr Munsfield?' Allegra addressed the patient gently.

'In…my stomach, and in my back…' he gasped and puffed. 'In the middle of my back… like a knife…'

Danielle arrived with the printouts, accompanied by Joel Addison, who had been collecting pathology reports from the printer. 'Hb is 80, white cell count 25 with neutrophilia, and his amylase and lipase are through the roof, Dr Tallis,' he said, looking intently through the sheath of figures before he met her eyes briefly. 'What do you feel is the problem?'

'Looks like we've got pancreatitis, maybe pancreatic sepsis. Could have an anastomotic leak,' Allegra said.

'I agree. We should also consider an anastomotic leak as the precipitating problem,' he suggested.

'Danielle, get the surgeon down here now. We need an urgent surgical review, and get X-ray up here, too—we need a chest X-ray. Those sats are worse. My guess is adult respiratory distress syndrome.'

'ARDS is almost certain, Dr Tallis. We'll need to intubate pretty much straight away but it's your call,' Joel said, giving her an unreadable look.

Allegra explained to the patient that there was a problem in his abdomen and that it was affecting his lungs, making it hard for him to breathe. She explained the procedure of intubation to him before instructing Fiona to obtain drugs and airway equipment.

'His Hb has dropped too, Dr Tallis,' Joel said, when she'd turned back from the patient. 'There are a couple of cross-matched units left over from surgery.' He turned to address Danielle. 'Can you retrieve those from the blood fridge while I help Dr Tallis here?'

After pre-oxygenating as much as possible, Allegra got Joel to inject 10mg suxamethonium and 10mg diazepam and applied a mask and bag.

'He's hard to inflate. His lungs are stiff with pulmonary oedema,' she said. 'I'll have to intubate him—he's too hard to keep bagging. Hand me the laryngoscope and tube, Dr Addison.'

Allegra introduced the laryngoscope and attempted intubation but the patient had only been extubated forty-eight hours before and the larynx was red and swollen. To make matters worse, he had a short, bullish neck. She couldn't see the cords and reverted to bag and mask, but could hardly keep a seal on the face with the mask because the insufflation pressure needed was so high.

She muttered a curse under her breath, conscious of Joel watching her every move. 'I'll have to try again. We're in real trouble here.'

'I can see that, but you're the most skilled here at airway management,' Joel said calmly. 'Just tell me how you want me to assist.'

Allegra threw him a quick grateful glance and tried the laryngoscope again but still could not intubate the patient. Mr Munsfield's sats were now 70 per cent and he was looking deeply cyanosed.

'We need to get an airway, Dr Tallis. He's badly hypoxic and throwing off VEBs,' Joel said.

'I can't get a tube in,' she said, her brow beading with perspiration. 'I'll have to do a surgical airway. Open the tray, Dr Addison, stat.'

Joel opened the surgical airway pack on the top of the trolley. Allegra put on sterile gloves and made a transverse incision over the cricothyroid membrane with a disposable scalpel. Taking a pair of artery forceps, she widened the hole, and passed in a cuffed tracheostomy tube and inflated the cuff, then connected the tube to the oxygen bag. The chest rose and fell with each pump on the bag, though the insufflation pressure was high.

Allegra flicked her gaze to the sats monitor, which showed the patient's sats coming up into the 90s. She connected the ventilator and set the dials to cope with the high pressure and poor oxygen exchange.

'Well done, Dr Tallis,' Joel said, briefly placing

a hand on her shoulder to steady her. 'That was a top-notch surgical airway under pressure. Things look back under control here. I'll leave you to fill Harry in—he's just arrived.'

He moved off towards the A and E area before Allegra could thank him for his help. She frowned as he went through the swing doors, her feelings towards him undergoing a confusing change which she couldn't quite explain.

The surgical registrar arrived with the consultant, Harry Upton, and was briefed by Allegra.

'He needs to be opened, I agree. The pancreatic anastomosis has probably leaked, and on top of that he's got pancreatitis. Thanks for salvaging the situation, Allegra.'

Danielle filled Harry in on the rest of the patient's details before he turned back to speak to Allegra. 'You look like you could do with a break.'

Allegra blew a wisp of damp hair off her face. 'I'm off for a break right now. It's been one of those mornings.'

'So you've finally met our new director,' Harry said with a twinkle in his eyes. 'I didn't see you at his welcome function last week.'

'I was on nights,' she explained, her mouth tightening a fraction.

Harry grinned at her sour expression. 'So what gives, Allegra? You don't like his…er…aura?'

She gave him a mock reproving look. 'Don't you start, Harry. He totally rubbished my project as if it was a load of pseudoscience. "Can't afford alternative therapies in his science-based unit", I think was how he put it.'

'Yeah, well, I guess he's under a lot of pressure to make this place work,' he said. 'There's a lot of cash been poured into it, and there are a few irate unit directors who think they should have got the funds instead. If it doesn't shape up fast, his head will roll.' He grimaced as his pager went off. 'I'm due in Theatre. I'll see you around. Good work on Mr Munsfield, by the way. You and Joel Addison make quite an impressive team.'

She gave him another mock reproving glance but a small smile softened it. 'Thanks, Harry.'

Allegra was using the staff restroom to freshen up when Kellie Wilton, one of her colleagues, came in.

'I was hoping I'd run into you,' Kellie said as she washed her hands at the basin. 'I heard about your meeting with Dr Addison.'

Allegra frowned as she twisted her light brown hair back into its clip. 'The hospital grapevine is running rampant again, I see,' she said, turning to look at her friend. 'Who told you about it?'

'Louise mentioned it at morning tea,' Kellie said, leaning back against the basin. 'It certainly sounds as if you got off on the wrong foot. What's his problem with your project? I thought Patrick Naylor was touting it as a unique study.'

'He did, but apparently Dr Addison is under the impression that *his* decisions bear more weight than those of the chief executive officer. I hate men with overblown egos and closed minds.'

'How is your relationship going with Patrick, by the way?'

Allegra put her hands on her hips and gave her friend a frustrated grimace. 'Listen, Kellie, I had dinner with him—once. It wasn't even in a posh restaurant and I ended up paying because his credit card wouldn't swipe. We had pizza and a bottle of awful red wine, which I was still paying for with a headache the next morning. He spent the whole time complaining about his soon-to-be-ex-wife. Hardly what I'd call a date.'

'Yeah, I'd heard his separation had hit him hard,' Kellie reflected. 'You do need to get out more, Allegra, with some fresh talent. Have you ever thought about using a dating service? My sister did and got a real honey.'

'I don't believe what I'm hearing, Kellie. What do you think—I'm desperate or something?' Allegra gaped at her. 'I can find my own dates without the help of a computer, thanks very much.'

'One bad dinner in two years is not a good track record,' Kellie pointed out.

'Eighteen months,' Allegra corrected her swiftly.

'Look, Allegra, you're twenty-eight years old. We've known each other a while now, and as far as I can tell the only fun you've had lately is sharing tubs of chocolate-chip ice cream with me while watching soppy movies at my place.'

Allegra sucked in her stomach and groaned. 'Don't remind me. It's taken me four weeks to get my jeans to do up again after the last time.'

Kellie smiled. 'Some of us are going to go out for drinks this evening after work. Why don't you join us?'

'Where are you going?'

'Just down to the pub on Elgin Street. It won't be a late night. You're not on call, are you?'

Allegra shook her head in relief. 'No, thank God.'

'So will you come?' Kellie urged. 'You never know, you might pick up.'

'What? A cold sore or a strep throat?'

Kellie laughed. 'You *are* a sad case, Allegra. You've been hanging around unconscious people way too long.'

'Maybe,' Allegra said with a wry smile. 'But they don't break your hearts and they're not unfaithful.'

Kellie's expression softened. 'And they don't always live, no matter how hard you try.' She placed a gentle hand on her friend's arm. 'Alice Greeson didn't have a chance, Allegra. You did your best.'

'I know…' Her shoulders slumped a little. 'But telling the family is always so hard. She was just twenty-one. I thought she was responding…'

'She was brain dead, Allegra,' Kellie said. 'It was hopeless right from the start. You did what you could but the brain injury she sustained in that car accident was beyond anything medical science could repair.'

Allegra gave a long sigh. 'I know, but I guess I was hoping for a miracle. They happen occasionally, I just so wanted one for Alice and her family.'

'You'll get your miracle one day,' Kellie said. 'We all do. It's what keeps us going. Why else would we work the hours we do if there were no miracles?'

Allegra smiled. 'You're right. Thanks, Kel. What time did you say drinks are on?'

'Just come when you've finished your shift. The place will be rocking by the time you get there so come no matter what time you finish. You need some chill-out time.'

'You sound like my mother.'

'Yes, well, mothers often know best, although I'm not sure mine would approve of the date I have lined up for the weekend.'

'Don't tell me you're doing that internet dating thing, like your sister?'

Kellie grinned. 'Why not? Look at her, six months on and she's married and pregnant to a gorgeous guy. It could happen to any of us.'

Allegra rolled her eyes. 'My mother would have a coronary if I told her I was dating someone I'd met on-line. My father would be even worse. They'd be doing a personality inventory and an astrology and numerology profile on the guy, and checking out his background with a private investigator. I think I'll have to do it the old-fashioned way, you know, boy meets girl, that sort of thing.'

'That sort of thing usually ends in divorce,' Kellie pointed out. 'Physical attraction is one thing but finding someone you can relate to is the stuff that really counts. You need to be friends first, lovers second.'

'Yeah…I guess you're right, but with the sort of hours I work, how am I going to find the time to make friends with anyone halfway decent? Most men expect you to sleep with them on the second or third date these days. They're not interested in friendship, they're interested in getting laid as soon as they can.'

'That's why the dating service is so useful,' Kellie said. 'It cuts corners for you by weeding out the weirdos and the ones who have no interests in common with you. Think about it. I can get Jessica to do a preliminary printout for you to show you how it works.'

'I'll think about it,' Allegra said, as she shouldered open the door. 'I'll see you tonight.'

The door swung shut behind her but halfway along the corridor she came face to face with Patrick.

'Hello, gorgeous,' he said, planting a moist kiss to her mouth before she could turn her head away in time.

'Patrick…I…' She tried to push herself away but his hands were heavy on her shoulders.

'Have dinner with me tonight?' he asked, his tone pleading.

She opened her mouth to respond when just past his right shoulder she caught sight of Joel, coming out of one of the smaller meeting rooms used for conferencing with the relatives of patients. His dark eyes were cynical and there was a hint of something that looked very much like a smirk at the corners of his mouth.

'Sorry, Patrick, but I promised Kellie I'd join some of the others for drinks later this evening,' she said. 'Maybe some other time.'

'I'll hold you to it,' he said, and, pressing another quick kiss to her mouth before she could avoid it, went on his way in the opposite direction.

Joel stepped away from the doorjamb he'd been leaning against and walked towards her, his eyes very dark as they held hers. 'Dr Tallis, no doubt you will disagree with me on principle, but perhaps it might be prudent to refrain from fraternising with members of staff in the corridors of the unit. I wouldn't want any of our patients' relatives to think that you're acting unprofessionally.'

'I wasn't acting unprofessionally, I was just—'

'Dr Tallis.' His low deep tone brooked no resistance as he pointed to the room he had left a short time ago. 'In that conference room are the parents of a young man who was admitted to ICTU a short time ago. He fell from a building site and has suspected spinal injuries. I do not think that they need to see right now two members of staff going for it in the corridor.'

She glared at him in affront. 'We were not going for—' But she cut herself short when out of the corner of her eye she saw the conference-room door open down the corridor. She watched in silence as a middle-aged couple came out with the head neuro-surgeon, Anthony Pardle, in attendance, their faces ravaged by the emotion they were going through on hearing of the extent of their son's injuries.

As much as Allegra wanted the last word, she knew it would be pointless. Joel had yet again stripped her of her professional dignity, and the last thing she wanted was for anyone else to witness it. She didn't understand why he had to be so obstructive. He had been so helpful with Mr Munsfield earlier, but now it looked as if the momentary truce was at an end.

She waited until the patient's parents and Anthony Pardle had passed before lowering her gaze and briefly apologising, even though the words felt like acid in her throat. 'I'm sorry. It won't happen again, Dr Addison.'

'Fine.'

Allegra felt the silent magnetic pull of his dark brown gaze, her breath stalling somewhere in the middle of her chest as their eyes locked. The silence was so thick she felt as if it was going to choke her. Her heart began to thump a little irregularly as his gaze slipped to her mouth for a nanosecond before returning to her wide green eyes.

'Fine…' he said again, running a hand through the thickness of his hair in a manner that appeared to Allegra to be slightly agitated. 'I'll…er…let you get back to work.'

She watched as he turned and walked with long purposeful strides up the length of the corridor, before disappearing from sight through the swing doors at the end.

She blew out a little uneven breath and gave herself a mental shake.

Don't even think about it, she scolded herself sternly. Dr Joel Addison was definitely in the 'too hard' basket. And for the sake of her heart he had better stay there.

CHAPTER THREE

THE pub was noisy and crowded by the time Allegra made her way there, but she wove her way through the clots of people to the table where some of the other Melbourne Memorial staff were sitting, chatting volubly over their drinks.

Kellie waved to her as she approached. 'Come and sit here, Allegra.' She made room for her on the booth seat. 'What will you have to drink?'

'I'd better start with something soft,' she said. 'After five nights of on-call my head for alcohol gets a little wonky. I'll have a lemon, lime and bitters, but you sit down—I'll get it. Do you want a top-up?'

'Thanks. Vodka and orange,' Kellie said.

Allegra made her way to the bar, saying a quick hello to two of the surgical registrars who'd been on call with her the last week. After a short exchange with them she carried the drinks back to the table where Kellie was and sat down with a sigh of relief marking the end of a stressful day.

'How's your coma study going, Allegra?' Margaret Hoffman, an anaesthetic registrar, asked.

Allegra exchanged a quick glance with Kellie before responding. 'The new director doesn't think it's scientific enough for his exacting standards. He's giving me a month to prove it's worthwhile.'

'Oh?' Margaret looked surprised. 'But it's all been approved and your work on the Greeson girl was worthwhile, I thought.'

'The Greeson girl died,' Allegra said with a despondent sigh.

'I know, but what you might not have realised at the time was how much it meant to her parents, having you there. I saw the way they drew comfort from you massaging their daughter's legs and arms, touching her like a real person, instead of someone who'd been written off as a vegetable. You gave them a lot of comfort in a tragic situation, Allegra. Even if the study achieves nothing for the patient, it sure as hell gives the relatives comfort—shows that the staff are treating their loved one with dignity, like a real person.'

'She's right, Allegra,' Kellie said. 'That's what's missing from medicine these days. The staff are all run off their feet, no one has time any more for simple things, like holding a patient's hand or listening to their worries or giving them a soothing back rub.'

'I guess you're right. But if I'm going to show anything from the study, I'm going to need the support of the director,' Allegra said, reaching for her drink. 'He seems against it on principle, and we haven't exactly had the best start to a working relationship.'

'I thought he was lovely when I met him at the welcome function,' Margaret said with a twinkle in her eye, 'and good-looking, too, which of course always helps.'

'I wouldn't care if he looked like the hunchback of Notre Dame as long as he lets me do my project—it's really important to me,' Allegra growled.

'Ah, but your involvement with Patrick Naylor gives you the trump card, surely,' Margaret said. 'I say, why not aim for the top if you can.'

Allegra frowned as she put down her drink. 'I'm not involved with Patrick. Not in any way. Who on earth starts these rumours?'

It was Margaret's turn to frown. 'But I heard him tell everyone in the doctors' room the other day how you had dinner together. He's really into you, Allegra. He made that very clear.'

'He's still officially married, for God's sake,' Allegra said. 'Besides, I'm not the slightest bit attracted to him.'

'Well, someone's definitely got their lines crossed,' Margaret said, as she leaned back in her seat. 'The way Patrick tells it, it sounds as if you are the reason his marriage split up in the first place.'

'*No!*' Allegra gasped. 'That's not true! I only went out with him as he seemed so down. It was more of a goodwill gesture. I was worried about him. He told me his wife had left him and he started to cry. I'm hopeless when men do that, it really gets to me. I just can't help going into rescue mode.'

'Uh-oh,' Kellie said, glancing towards the bar. 'Don't look now but guess who just walked in?'

Allegra groaned and put her head in her hands. 'Please, don't let it be Patrick Naylor. I just couldn't bear it.'

'It's not Patrick.'

Allegra lifted her head out of her hands and swivelled in her chair to see Joel looking straight at her. She turned back to her drink, her face feeling hot all of a sudden.

'Guess who's blushing,' Kellie teased, and, leaning closer, whispered, 'Go on, admit it, Allegra, he's hot. Look at those biceps—he must be lifting bull-dozers in the gym.'

'Shut up—he'll hear you,' she muttered hoarsely.

'He's coming over,' Kellie said. 'Hello, Dr Addison. There's a spare seat over here opposite Allegra.'

Allegra stifled a groan and sent her friend a blistering glare.

'Thanks,' Joel said, taking the seat facing Allegra. 'Can I get anyone a fresh drink?'

'I'm fine, thanks,' Margaret said with a friendly smile.

'Me, too,' Kellie said. Giving Margaret a surreptitious nudge, she got to her feet. 'We're calling it a night anyway. We're on early, aren't we, Margi?'

'Are we? Oh, yes…silly me.' Margaret grinned sheepishly and wriggled out of the booth. 'See you later.'

Allegra would have sent another scorching glare her friend's way but Joel's dark gaze had already searched for and located hers.

'What about you, Dr Tallis?' he asked, once the girls had left. 'What's your poison?'

'I'm only drinking soft this evening,' she said, her eyes falling away from his.

'On call?'

'No.'

A small silence tightened the air.

'I hope I didn't frighten your friends away,' he said after a moment. 'They seemed in a hurry to leave once I arrived.'

Her eyes came back to his, her expression taut with resentment. 'They were trying to set us up. Surely you could see that?'

He frowned in puzzlement. 'Set us up? What do you mean?'

She resisted the urge to roll her eyes. What planet had he just come down from?

'Set up as in matchmake,' she explained with a disapproving grimace. 'Kellie does it all the time. It drives me nuts.'

Joel took a leisurely sip of his lime and soda as he studied her expression. She had a wry twist to her mouth, as if the thought of being connected to him in any way was impossible.

'I take it she doesn't approve of your relationship with the CEO?' he inserted into the silence.

'I am *not* having a relationship with the CEO.' She bit out each word with determination.

'So that little tableau I witnessed earlier today was an aberration of some sort?'

'Patrick and I are friends…sort of…' she said.

'He's going through a particularly acrimonious separation. I found myself lending an ear one day and now it seems the hospital is rife with the rumours of us being involved. Nothing could be further from the truth.'

'Hospitals are like that. Members of staff have only to stop and talk in the corridor and everyone thinks something's going on,' he commented. 'But perhaps you should be straight with him. He seems to think you're his for the taking.'

Allegra frowned. 'I know…but I don't know how to avoid hurting his feelings.'

Joel finished his drink. 'He'll get over it. Tell him you're involved with someone else.'

'Yeah, right, like who?' she said, with another rueful twist to her mouth. 'I work thirteen-hour shifts. I don't even have time to do my own laundry and shopping, let alone find a date.'

'I know what you mean,' he said with a wry smile. 'I haven't had a date in a year and a half. My mother is threatening to register me on an internet dating service.'

Allegra stared at him.

'What's wrong?' he asked. 'What did I say?'

She gave her head a little shake and picked up her almost empty glass for something to do to occupy her hands. 'Nothing… It's just that Kellie was suggesting I do the same.'

'When you think about it, it sounds good in theory.'

She scrunched up her face in scepticism. 'You think so?'

'Yeah.' He leaned back in his seat, one arm lying casually along the back of the booth. 'It cuts the chaff from the wheat, if you know what I mean.'

Allegra couldn't stop a bubble of laughter escaping her lips. '*Chaff and wheat?* Is that how guys these days refer to women?'

He gave her an answering smile. 'I guess it's not the best metaphor, but I thought sheep and goats would probably be worse.'

'You could be right,' she said, still smiling.

Joel ran his eyes over her features, taking in the light brown slightly wavy hair that seemed to be protesting about being restrained at the back of her head with a clip of some sort; loose tendrils were falling out around her small ears, and one long strand was over one of her rainforest green eyes. He watched as she tucked it behind her ear with her small slim fingers, her nails short but neat. Her face was faintly shadowed with residual tiredness but he knew if he looked in a mirror right now, his would look very much the same. Her mouth was soft and full, and her skin creamy white, as if she hadn't seen much of Melbourne's hot summer.

She looked like she worked hard and he felt a little uncomfortable with how he had spoken to her earlier. She had a good reputation among the staff, everyone spoke highly of her dedication to patients, but he couldn't help feeling her project had all the potential to provoke criticism and crackpot commentary as the new ICTU was evaluated by those who had backed its funding and those who had lost out on their own funding as a result. From what he'd heard so far, her study was time-consuming, had little theoretical basis and it would be hard to show results. And he of all people knew how important results were. His parents' situation was living proof of how the wrong results could change everything—for ever.

'So...' Allegra said, moistening her lips as she searched for something to fill the silence. 'How are you enjoying things so far at Melbourne Memorial?'

'It's a great facility,' he answered, 'the first of its kind in Australia. Having Trauma Reception on the same floor as ICU means that ICU staff are at close hand to be involved with trauma management. It's a very innovative concept, even for a level-3 trauma centre.'

'Yes, it makes a lot of sense. Less handing over of patients from one group to another, involvement of ICU staff right from the start of resus, and less movement of patients, too,' Allegra agreed. 'Wheeling patients twenty metres straight into ICU, instead of the old arrangement of up two floors and the opposite end of the hospital is a huge plus in itself.'

'And having the two fully equipped operating theatres in Trauma Reception is real cutting edge,' Joel said, 'although some of the surgeons and theatre staff I've spoken to haven't been too keen on it, actually. They don't like splitting the staff and equipment between the main theatre and us.'

'It can be disorientating, working in an unfamiliar theatre,' Allegra pointed out, in the surgeons' defense.

He held her gaze for a moment. 'There are some good people here. But it's a high-pressure job and I'm very conscious of being the new broom, so to speak.'

'You really like your metaphors, don't you?'

His smile was crooked. 'I do, don't I?'

Allegra found the friendly, more approachable side to him totally refreshing and wondered if he was trying to make up for the bad start they'd had. Without the stark backdrop of the hospital and without his white coat and tie, he looked like any other good-looking guy in his early to mid-thirties. His face was marked by fatigue but, looking around the bar, most of the hospital staff who were still here looked much the same. It came with the job. Chronic tiredness was a given, especially in ICU, where the shifts were long and the work intense.

'I heard you've been working overseas,' she said, toying with the straw in her empty glass.

Joel's eyes went to her hands before returning to her face. 'Would you like another drink?'

'Um…why not?' she said, deciding she was starting to enjoy herself for the first time in ages. 'Vodka and lime.'

'Coming up,' he said, and got up to get their drinks.

He came back and, placing her drink in front of her, took his seat opposite. 'Yes, I was overseas for a while.' He returned to her earlier question, his expression clouding a fraction.

'Where were you stationed?'

'In the Middle East.'

'That would have been tough, I imagine.'

He took a sip of his drink before answering. 'Yeah, it was.'

Allegra could sense he didn't want to talk about it in any detail and wondered if he'd been involved in any of the skirmishes that had seen countless people injured or maimed for life.

She took another sip of her drink and changed the subject. 'Are you a Melbourne boy?'

'Yep, born and bred. What about you?'

'I'm a bit of a crossbreed, I'm afraid,' she said. 'My father is originally from Sydney and my mother is a Melbourne girl. They both live here now but not together. I've spent equal amounts of time with them over the years.'

'They're divorced?'

'They never married in the first place,' she said. 'But they're the best of friends. They never went down that blame-game route. They're what you might call…progressive.'

'Progressive?'

'They have a sort of open relationship. They don't live together but whenever my mum needs a partner for some function or other, she takes my dad, and vice versa.' She gave him a little embarrassed glance and added, 'I wouldn't be surprised if they still occasionally sleep together.'

'You're right,' he said. 'That's pretty progressive.'

'What about you?' she asked, picking up her glass. 'Are your parents still together?'

'Yes, for something like thirty-five years.'

'Do you have any brothers or sisters?'

His eyes moved away from hers as he reached for his glass, absently running the tips of two of his fingers through the beads of condensation around the sides. 'I have a twin brother.'

There was something about his tone that alerted Allegra to an undercurrent of emotion. His expression was now shuttered, as if he regretted allowing the conversation to drift into such personal territory.

'Are you identical?' she ventured.

'Yes and no.'

Allegra frowned at his noncommittal answer but before she could think of a response to it he met her eyes and asked, 'What do your parents do for a living?'

'My father's a psychologist, who specialises in dream therapy, and my mother is a Tai Chi and yoga instructor.'

His eyebrows rose slightly. 'No wonder you have a tendency towards the other-worldly.'

'I would hardly call what I do *that*,' she protested, with a reproving glance.

'So what exactly is it you do?' he asked, settling back into his seat once more.

'You'll only rubbish it so what would be the point?'

'I promise to listen without comment,' he said.

'Look, right now we're just two overworked, tired people in a bar, chatting over a drink, OK?'

She let out a tiny sigh after a moment's hesitation. 'All right.' She took a little breath and briefly explained her theory of how human sensory touch could strongly trigger memories that might be integral to stimulating consciousness in a comatose patient. 'There is evidence that skin sensation is wired up as our most primitive memory system, plugging more directly into primitive brain areas. If you think about your dreams, and record them after you wake up, the sensations you were experiencing just before you woke up are nearly always touch-related sensations. So—in this study, I encourage the relatives, particularly those who are most intimately involved with the patient, to touch them in predetermined ways. I teach them how to massage and touch their loved one in ways we think will trigger strong memories.'

Joel remained silent as she talked passionately about some of the trials she'd done, including one involving a post-heart-surgery coma patient.

'It was striking,' she said. 'The relatives were advised to consider turning off his life support. There was virtually no sign of brain activity. But then his wife told me their daughter was flying back from Canada to say goodbye to him. She hadn't seen him in fifteen years. When she arrived I got her to touch him on his eyebrows, nose and lips and talk to him just like she did when she was a child and he used to put her to bed with this little routine. His eyes opened, he looked directly at his daughter's eyes for about thirty seconds, and then a few minutes later died peacefully.'

'So he didn't recover.'

Allegra tried not to be put off by the inherent cynicism in his tone. 'No, but that's not the point. He woke up in time to say goodbye. He recognised his daughter's touch—some powerful memory was triggered that induced momentary consciousness.'

'There's no way of testing that scientifically,' he pointed out.

'I realise it's just one case, and there was no measurement of brain activity being done on him. But that's the whole point of my study now—to get some measurements of these effects. And other triggers, too. Some of the other therapies I use involve other body memories, such as smell and sound. Haven't you ever heard a piece of music and found it took you back to a time that was significant to you? Music stirs emotions, so do certain aromas. And emotional memories are the most powerful, centred in the amygdala of the brain. The so-called healing properties of essential oils such as neroli, Roman chamomile, frankincense, bergamot, clary sage may have more to do with how they neurologically trigger emotional memory.'

'Yes, but none of these are controlled substances—they could have contaminants. There are cases where clary sage used topically by pregnant women were associated with birth defects. Peppermint oil can trigger epilepsy. My concern is that you are introducing therapies into a high-tech area that have never been through any approval or evaluation process. If there was even the suggestion of some adverse reaction, we'd be crucified.'

'I'm following strict guidelines—they've been approved by the ethics and research committees. My goal is to make a substantial breakthrough in coma recovery. I don't want to be stopped by closed-minded bureaucracy.'

'I suppose by that comment you're referring to me.'

'Well, you've hardly been encouraging,' she said with a hint of pique.

'It's not my job to win a popularity contest. I have to run this new and very expensive department according to the guidelines laid down in my contract. And it boils down to, one, dollars and cents, keeping within the budget. And, two, best practice, with significant benefits from the expense of the new layout. I can't be seen to be dabbling in pseudoscience with hard fought-over hospital money.'

'So you still think it's a worthless enterprise to touch a person who is ill or dying, or in a coma, do you?' she asked, unable to remove the stringency from her tone. 'For relatives and friends to spend hours by their bedside, holding their hand, stroking them and telling them how much they love them?'

He frowned at her censure. 'No, of course not. It's just that ICTU is cluttered enough as it is. It's not the place or the right time to bring in alternative therapists and their potions and sounds. And think of the increased risk of infection if people came and went all the time without proper regulation.'

'I don't often introduce other therapists,' she said. 'I do most of the work myself.'

'So you've got a degree in quackery as well as medicine, have you? What a busy little bee you have been over the last few years.'

Allegra got to her feet in one stiff movement, her expression tight with anger. 'You know something, Dr Addison? It's just as well you weren't recruited for a popularity contest because if it was up to me, you wouldn't have got past the first round of selection criteria.'

'And what criteria would they be, I wonder?' he asked, with a little curl of his lip. 'Perhaps my aura isn't giving off the right vibes or maybe my office doesn't have the right Feng Shui. Perhaps you should make an appointment with me to rearrange it for me.'

She pressed her hands on the table and leaned across so the other people close by couldn't hear, her green eyes flashing with anger. 'The only things I'd like to rearrange are your attitude and personality, and if there wasn't a law against it, I'd like to apply some touch therapy to your face as well—in the form of a very hard slap.'

His dark eyes glittered as they held hers. 'Go right ahead, sweetheart, and see how quickly you get fired from the department.'

'You can't fire me,' she spat back defiantly. 'Patrick Naylor does the hiring and firing.'

He got to his feet, his sudden increase in height making her shrink back in intimidation. 'I can assure you, Dr Tallis, that it would take just one word from me and the CEO will tear up your contract and your project into a thousand pieces,' he said, and with one last glowering look brushed past her and left.

CHAPTER FOUR

'So how was your little drink last night with the director?' Louise asked in the female staff change room the next morning.

Allegra scowled as she thrust her handbag into her locker and turned the key with a savage twist of her hand. 'I'm going to kill Kellie Wilton and Margaret Hoffman.'

'So he didn't invite you back to his place for coffee, then?'

'No, he did not. He threatened to have me fired, that's what he did.'

'Fired! Can he do that?' Louise asked. 'I thought the CEO was the only one who could hire or fire?'

'I'm beginning to think Joel Addison could do anything if he put his mind to it.'

'It's tough, being at the top, Allegra,' Louise pointed out reasonably. 'There's been a lot of opposition about the refurbishment being so innovative and all. Dr Addison is probably being overly cautious, which is perfectly understandable. You know the fuss the surgeons made about the new trauma theatre locations. If this unit doesn't produce results and come in on budget, Dr Addison's the one who will take the rap.'

'I know all that,' Allegra said, pocketing her locker key and turning to face Louise. 'You know, for a while there last night I was starting to see a glimpse of a nice sort of man. He was chatty and seemed interested in what I had to say.'

'So what happened?'

She gave a frustrated up-and-down movement of her shoulders. 'Who knows? He just seems to really have it in for anyone a little to the left of what he believes is scientific. It's as if it's a personal agenda or something.'

'Maybe someone in the past gave him a lousy massage,' Louise said with a little grin.

Allegra rolled her eyes. 'The only thing he wants massaged is his ego, but I for one am not going to do it.'

'Have you told him your personal reasons for being so committed to your project?'

Allegra blew out a breath and leaned back against the lockers with a noisy rattle. 'No… If I did, it would only make things worse. He'd only say I was looking through an emotional lens instead of a scientific one.'

'But it might help him understand why it's so important to you if you tell him what happened to your friend in med school,' Louise said gently.

Allegra pushed herself away from the lockers as her beeper sounded. 'Look, I've put what happened to Julie behind me. I can't allow myself to dwell on it. It won't change anything. But I owe it to her memory to stop it happening again and, so help me, God, Dr Addison had better not try and stop me.'

She made her way quickly to the trauma centre sandwiched between the ambulance bay and the main ICTU. Two trauma bays were in operation when she arrived, ambulance personnel, including two crews of Heli Flight Retrieval Paramedics intermingling with the A and E medical and nursing staff.

'What's going on?' Allegra asked Alex Beswin, the A and E senior staffer, as she reached the scene of flurried activity.

'Hi, Allegra. Two people brought in from the Victorian Alps after a single vehicle accident. Seems their car went off the side of the road and ended up in the river. A car travelling behind stopped and the driver managed to get the mother and the kid in the car free, but both were unconscious and spent a bit of time in the cold water until the rescue team arrived to haul them out. The kid is still unconscious and still hypothermic and bradycardic. The mother has been rewarmed, but she has head injuries, a flail chest and blunt abdo trauma. We need your help on the boy—he was tubed at the scene but the airway's not great and he'll need to go up to CT soon. Joel Addison is heading the team getting the mother under control—she's going to CT now. They'll both need ICTU after we've finished here.'

'Right,' Allegra said, heading for bay one, where the small child was contained.

Tony Ringer, one of the A and E staff consultants, who was directing the care there, looked up in obvious relief when Allegra appeared at the foot of the bed.

'Allegra, listen—this tube's in too far, it's too small and there are anterior neck injuries from the air bag. We need to change it but I'd be grateful if you would do it. I'll help.'

Allegra moved to the head of the bed and, taking the airway bag and checking the tube and connectors, she listened to the chest with her stethoscope. 'Yes, you're right, Tony. The left side's not inflating, the tube is too small and probably down the right main bronchus. We'll change it for a six point five but we need to be ready for a surgical airway if his larynx is oedematous. I'll change the tube over an introducer to maintain access.'

Tony took over bagging the child while Allegra, with the help of one of the nursing staff, arranged all the equipment she needed, setting it out for easy access.

'Right, Tony, let's do it,' Allegra said, taking a breath to steady herself.

She took a long flexible plastic introducer and, after disconnecting the endotracheal tube from the bag, passed the introducer into the ETT and the right main bronchus. She then deflated the ETT cuff and pulled the tube out of the airway and over the introducer. She rapidly passed a cuffed 6.5 ETT back over the introducer and into the trachea with not much difficulty, positioning the tube this time in the trachea so that both lungs would be inflated, and blew up the cuff. She checked the insufflation of both lungs with her stethoscope and, satisfied that the tube was in the correct position, secured it with tape.

'Good job, Allegra,' Tony said. 'It's a godsend, having someone with increased airway skills for this sort of situation.'

'Thanks, Tony. I guess that's a benefit of the anaesthetic rotation through ICTU.'

'True,' Tony replied. 'Listen, this kid's still hypothermic. We're running in warmed intraperitoneal saline now, and as soon as his temperature is up we'll need to get him next door for a head CT. Can you manage the airway for his transfer and then settle him into ICTU for us? I want to look over the second team treating the mother. And word's just through that the husband and father has just been located. He's on his way in.'

'What's the boy's name?' Allegra asked.

'Tommy Lowe,' Tony answered. 'I don't know his age, his father was too distressed to talk. What do you think?'

Allegra looked at the tiny body on the bed with tubes running out of him, her stomach clenching in distress that someone so young had had to suffer so much. 'I reckon he's about six or seven.'

'Too young for this sort of caper,' Tony said, stripping off his gloves and tossing them in the bin.

'Tell me about it,' Allegra said. Stripping off her own gloves, she reached out with a gentle hand and touched the little boy on his arm, her fingers soft and warm on his cold pale limb.

Joel was in ICTU, finishing setting the mother up on a ventilator, when Allegra brought the little boy Tommy round from CT.

'CT on the mother shows some contusion, but no intracranial haemorrhage,' he said, glancing at her briefly, his expression coolly professional, showing no trace of his anger of the night before. 'She's got a flail chest on the right and underlying contusion. She had an intercostal tube put in before they transferred her. I've just had to retape the connectors, otherwise that's OK. Her abdo CT shows a liver contusion, but no free blood, so the surgeons are treating it expectantly at this stage. She'll have another CT tomorrow. Her bloods were pretty normal, the Hb down as expected. But there was one unexpected finding, about which we'll have to inform the police.'

'What's that?' she asked, as she supervised the transfer of Tommy from the trolley to the ICTU bed.

'Her blood alcohol is through the roof—point one. No wonder she ran off the road.'

'That's unbelievable!' Allegra said. 'How could a mother drive along a winding mountainous road with a child in the car, having drunk herself stupid?'

'I'm sending off a drug test as well,' he said with a grim set to his mouth. 'I have a bad gut feeling about this scenario. Something else is going on, maybe suicide—actually, a murder-suicide.'

Allegra felt a cold shiver of unease pass through her as she looked at the woman hooked up to the ventilator. What circumstances in her life would cause her to take that drastic step?

'What about the boy?' Joel asked. 'Any results from the CT?'

'No detectable macro brain injury. He could have general minor contusion, maybe slight cerebral oedema. His core temp's up to 37 now. No other major injuries. We ran the scanner over his neck, chest and abdo—all clear,' Allegra reported.

Danielle Capper appeared. 'Dr Addison? Dr Tallis? Mrs Lowe's husband is here. Perhaps you should speak to him before he comes in. He's very agitated. I've made him a cup of tea and he's in conference room two.'

Joel helped Allegra set Tommy up on the ventilator then while Allegra set up the IV lines with the nursing staff, Joel removed the intraperitoneal catheter, which had been used to rewarm the patient, stripped off his gloves and exchanged a quick glance with Allegra. 'We'd better talk to the father together.'

'Right,' she agreed, mentally bracing herself. How would the father of the little boy cope with hearing his wife had been driving under the influence, let alone if what Joel suspected was true—that she'd done so deliberately in an attempt to kill herself and her child?

Joel opened the conference-room door to find a man in his mid to late thirties pacing the floor, his face haggard, his clothes looking as if he'd just thrown them on haphazardly. His tie was hanging loosely and his shirt buttons were done up crookedly.

'I want to see my son! Where is he?'

'Mr Lowe, I'm Dr Joel Addison and this Dr Allegra Tallis. Your son is in ICTU—we've just stabilised him.'

'And my wife?' Mr Lowe asked, his hands tightening by his sides.

'She's also in the unit,' Joel said. 'Both she and your son are being ventilated with a machine to help with breathing. They both have head injuries. We're not sure yet about how severe those injuries are. The neurosurgical team is coming down now, and will almost certainly want to do a minor procedure on each to insert a pressure monitor. We'll have a lot better idea when that's in, and also with a period of observation.'

'She was drinking, wasn't she?' Mr Lowe said through clenched teeth. He swung away and turned with his back to them and looked out of the window, which overlooked the hospital garden.

'I know this has been a terrible shock for you, Mr Lowe,' Allegra said gently, 'but if you're up to it now, can we ask you a few questions to help us with planning management before we take you in to see them?'

He turned around and with a heavy sigh took the nearest chair and collapsed into it, his head going to his hands.

Joel waited until Allegra was seated before he took the other chair. 'Mr Lowe, your wife had a blood alcohol level of point one—that's double the legal limit for driving. Was she taking any medication that you were aware of?'

Mr Lowe lifted his head out of his hands and looked at Joel through red-rimmed eyes. 'She's been on antidepressants for six months.' His eyes shifted away to look down at his hands. 'And drinking on and off for a few weeks. But I never thought she'd do something like this…'

'You think she crashed the car deliberately?' Allegra asked.

Keith Lowe looked at her with a grim expression

tightening his mouth. 'We've been having some…
trouble…in the relationship. I was trying to work
things out with her. I suggested counselling, but she
wouldn't hear of it. This supposed disaster of a
holiday in the mountains was my idea to try and
patch things up. She was against it, of course…but
she eventually agreed to come. I had some business
in town to see to so she and Tommy drove up first.
I was to join them later.' He rubbed at his jaw and
added, 'If I'd suspected this was what was going
through her head, I would never have allowed her
to go…'

'Has she ever shown suicidal tendencies before?'
Joel asked.

'No, not really, just troughs of depression. She'd
sit around the house and do nothing…for weeks at
a time and then snap out of it.' He ran a hand
through his coarse, wiry hair. 'It's been a living
hell, I can tell you. But I had to stick it out…if for
nothing else than for Tommy's sake.'

'Yes, of course,' Joel said. 'Would you like to
see them now?'

'Yes…' The man's eyes moistened. 'I want to see
that Tommy's alive…' He choked back a sob and
Allegra silently handed him the box of tissues from
one of the side tables.

'Try not to be put off by the tubes and machin-
ery—it's all support equipment to keep things stabilised while we watch for improvement. I know
how terrifying it all looks. He's young and strong—
I know having his father by his side will help him.'

Keith blew his nose and wiped at his eyes before
turning to Joel. 'I'd rather not see my wife right
now, if you don't mind. Not after…this….'

Joel got to his feet and placed a reassuring hand
on the man's shoulder. 'We understand. She's in the
next cubicle but I'll make sure the curtain is pulled
across between them. We can move them apart if
you can't cope.'

Mr Lowe appeared to think about it for a
moment. 'No…no…you don't have to do that. I
guess Tommy would want her near… I'll manage.'

'There are staff in constant attendance in ICTU,'
Allegra said. 'You can ring and talk to the one
looking after Tommy at any time.'

'How badly injured is my…wife?' he asked after
a tiny pause.

Joel answered. 'Well, apart from a head injury,
which is why she's unconscious at present, she has
broken ribs, some bruising of a lung and bruising
of her liver. She has a plastic drain in the chest to
keep the lungs inflated. The liver injury seems

stable, it probably won't need any surgery. And she has bruising around both upper arms, maybe where someone grabbed her to pull her out of the car, and in the middle of her back, maybe from prolonged pressure on the spine board during the transfer. She's deeply unconscious,' Joel said. 'It will be a few hours before we can get all the test results back.'

Mr Lowe's eyes shifted again. 'Is…?' He cleared his throat and continued, 'Is she expected to live?'

'She's in a serious condition but she's stable. We're giving her maximal supportive therapy. I think there's a fair chance for recovery,' Joel said.

Allegra stood to one side a few minutes later as Keith stood by his son's bed. She could see the up-and-down movement of his throat as he swallowed the rising emotion, and her chest felt uncomfortably tight at what he must be going through. How many times had she seen scenes just like this? Too many to recall, but this had to be one of the most tragic. Car accidents were horrific enough, without a suicide or murder motive attached.

'You can talk to him, Mr Lowe,' she said. 'Touch him and speak to him as much as you like.'

Keith Lowe kept his eyes trained on his little son. 'But he can't hear me, can he?'

'He is unconscious but that doesn't necessarily mean his brain won't register the sound of a very familiar voice. Your touch, too, is part of that memory process.'

Keith reached out a hand and placed it tentatively on his son's leg. He opened his mouth to speak but closed it again. Removing his hand from the boy's leg, he moved away from the bed, his expression tortured as he faced Allegra. 'I can't do this… I need to get some…air… I'm sorry… I can't cope with seeing him like this…'

'It's all right, Mr Lowe,' Allegra said softly.

His eyes spouted tears as he ground out bitterly. 'How can you possibly understand? That is my son lying there because that bitch behind that curtain put him there. If anyone deserves to die, it's her, not him. He's only seven years old, for God's sake!'

'Mr Lowe, I think it would be best if—'

'Excuse me.' Keith brushed past Allegra roughly and left the unit, ripping off the white protective surgical gown all visitors were required to wear in ICTU and tossing it roughly in the vague direction of the laundry bin.

'Dr Tallis?'

Allegra let out a little sigh and turned to face Joel, who had been attending to another patient nearby. 'Yes?'

'I'd like a word with you if you're free,' he said, 'in my office. No hurry. Just come when you get a spare moment.'

'I'm free now.'

'Good,' he said, moving past to shoulder open the swing doors. 'I'll have some coffee sent up.'

Louise sent Allegra a musing glance once the doors had closed on Joel's exit. 'Coffee or an olive branch, I wonder?'

Allegra rolled her lips together for a moment, her eyes on the small child lying so lifeless on the bed, only the hiss and groan of the ventilator breaking the silence.

'Allegra?' Louise gave her a little prod. 'Are you OK?'

She blinked and, giving her head a little shake, gave Louise a crooked smile. 'Sorry, I was miles away. Did you say something?'

'Nothing important,' Louise answered. 'But you'd better go and have that coffee with the director. You look like you need it.'

'Yes…' she said, and made her way out of ICTU to Joel's office a few doors down the corridor, a tiny frown taking up residence on her forehead.

CHAPTER FIVE

'COME in,' Joel called at Allegra's knock a short time later.

She came in and found him taking two cups of coffee off a tray, the fragrant aroma instantly teasing her nostrils.

'Quite a day,' he said, handing her a cup. 'Do you take milk or sugar?'

She shook her head. 'No, straight up is fine.'

Joel waited until she sat down before he took his chair behind his desk. His dark chocolate gaze connected with hers, the edge of his mouth tilted slightly. 'I suppose you're wondering why I've asked you to see me after what occurred between us last night.'

Allegra felt her colour rise but there was nothing she could do to stop it. 'As you said during the course of that…er…unfortunate conversation, we were two tired, overworked people, having a drink.'

There was a surprising level of warmth in his gaze as it held hers. 'Yes, that's true, but I still thought I should apologise, for being so…' He seemed to be hunting for a suitable word so she supplied it for him.

'Overbearing?'

He gave a soft chuckle of laughter, the sound of it sending a river of tiny feathery sensations down Allegra's spine. His eyes crinkled at the corners and his whole face softened, the tension and guardedness she was so used to seeing there now completely gone.

'I've been described as a lot of things in the past but "overbearing" is a first,' he said.

She arched one of her brows sceptically. 'Really? I'm surprised.'

His smile faded a little and he put down his cup. 'Look, Allegra, I know we haven't had a great start to our working relationship but I wanted to apologise for my part in last night's…er…unfortunate conversation, as you called it. I have no intention of speaking to Patrick Naylor about you. From what I've seen, you are a very competent anaesthetist with a high level of compassion for patients.'

'Thank you…'

'However, I did want to advise you about your handling of Keith Lowe.'

Allegra felt herself stiffen. 'Oh?'

'He's still in shock over what's happened. Also, I don't think he's the touchy-feely sort. A lot of men aren't. I was watching from bed four. He seemed very stiff and uncomfortable at touching the child.'

She frowned at him. 'So what are you saying?'

'I think it would be wise to go slowly with him in regard to your coma recovery plan. Somehow Keith Lowe doesn't strike me as a man who would be comfortable singing lullabies to his kid, no matter what the circumstances.'

'I wasn't thinking along the lines of lullabies, but I do think it's important Mr Lowe speaks to his son at the very least.'

'True. I agree. But the man's trying to come to terms with the as yet unanswered question of whether or not his wife tried to do herself in and take the child with her. To make matters worse, Kate is one bed away. He's edgy and very uncomfortable.'

'You think we should move her—maybe to one of the isolation rooms?'

Joel drummed his fingers on the desk for a moment. 'It's a thought…but, no, I think the transfer might be interpreted the wrong way. The father's already agreed Tommy might benefit from having his mother nearby.'

'Even though she tried to kill him?'

His eyes came back to hers. 'We don't know that. It could have been an accident.'

'You mean, straight driving under the influence?' she said. 'Driving with point one alcohol in the blood is hardly responsible behaviour for anyone, let alone a mother with a small child in the car.'

'Look, I know I brought up the suspicions in the first place, but it's probably wise not to make any judgements until we have more facts.'

'But Mr Lowe said she had a history of depression and he immediately assumed she'd been drinking, as if it was a regular occurrence.'

'Lots of people suffer periods of depression without trying to take their own or other's lives,' he pointed out.

'So why did you order a drug test? You must be more than a little suspicious.'

He let out a sigh and ran his hand through his hair. 'I just thought it best to make sure either way.' He glanced at his watch. 'The results should be in now.'

'What do you think they'll show?'

'One would assume she's been taking her anti-depressant, so that will show up—but at what level? And any other drugs—sedatives, tranquillisers. Maybe she took a cocktail of things.' He reached for the telephone and dialled the pathology department.

Allegra sipped her coffee and listened as he discussed the results with the lab.

'That high, huh? Both of them?' He raised his brows at Allegra. 'Yeah, I guess so. Right, thanks for speeding it through. The police will want a copy. I'll get them to contact you themselves— they may have their own questions.'

He put the phone down and sent Allegra a grave look. 'Mrs Lowe was on a cocktail of three drugs. Paroxetine at five times the maximum therapeutic level, diazepam at a high level and traces of codeine.'

'So she was really serious about doing it properly,' she said, starting to chew at her bottom lip.

'Looks more like it now.'

Allegra's frown increased. 'That's three drugs. You said "both of them". What exactly did you mean by that?'

'I wasn't referring to the number of drugs. I had the lab examine the boy's blood as well. It now seems that he had detectable diazepam as well, but not as high as hers.'

'What! She sedated the boy first?' she gasped in shock.

'That's what it looks like. Hard to believe

someone would do such a thing, but it's not the first time a parent has taken things to such extremes.'

'It's just so awful to think that if that car hadn't been behind them they would have died for sure…' she said, staring down at her hands.

'Maybe it was meant to happen this way.'

She looked up at that. 'What? Don't tell me the incredibly scientific Dr Joel Addison actually believes in something as metaphysical as destiny?'

He leaned back in his chair and studied her for a lengthy moment before asking, 'What have you got planned for the rest of the evening?'

She gave him a startled look. 'Planned?'

'After you finish work,' he said. 'What have you got planned?'

'Um…well, nothing really. I should do some washing, I guess. My machine broke down and my shifts have made it impossible for me to be there for the technician, but I can tell you the thought of sitting in a hot laundromat isn't too appealing.'

His smile relaxed his features again. 'So if I offered to take you out to dinner I might be in for a chance at you accepting, given the competition being so poor?'

Allegra felt her stomach do a funny little flip-flop. 'You're asking *me* to dinner?'

'You sound surprised.'

'I am.'

'Don't you get dinner invitations very often?'

She gave him a rueful look. 'Only from recently separated men who do nothing but whinge about their soon-to-be-ex-wives the whole time.'

'Well, I can assure I'm not married or separated or involved with anyone at present, much to my mother's ongoing disappointment.'

'You could always try internet dating,' she suggested with a tiny wry smile.

'I thought I might try this way first,' he said, and pushing out his chair got to his feet. 'That's if the laundromat isn't a better offer.'

Allegra stood up as well, wondering why her legs felt so wobbly and strange all of a sudden. 'It's close…but I suppose as long as you don't offer me pizza and cheap red wine, you're a marginally better prospect than the laundromat.'

'Marginally, eh?' He smiled as he held the door open for her. 'I'll pick you up at eight or is that too early?'

'No, but I haven't even given you my address.'

'Good point.' He reached for a pen and paper and she rattled off her street and apartment block number and watched as he wrote it down in a strong forceful script which she knew her mother would have a field day interpreting.

'See you tonight, then,' he said, pocketing the note.

'Yes… Thanks for the coffee.'

'You're welcome.'

She felt the pull of his gaze for several long seconds before she dragged hers away to walk through the door and down the corridor on legs that still felt as if someone had taken out the bones, just leaving the marrow…

Allegra checked on Tommy Lowe before she left for the evening. The neurosurgeons were planning insertion of intracranial pressure monitors on both him and his mother that night in the ICTU theatre. Susie, the ICU nurse looking after Tommy, reported all his obs stable, and the same for Kate, who she was also temporarily attending whilst Chloe, Kate's nurse, was out at tea.

'Poor little chap,' Susie said. 'How could a mother do that to an innocent child?'

Allegra wrote up the notes and handed the nurse the chart. 'It seems unbelievable, doesn't it? Mind you, it's still speculation so far, so better not to spread rumours we might regret later.'

'I hate the thought of even going near her,' Susie

confessed. 'I can't wait for Chloe to come back from her break.'

'We've got to treat Mrs Lowe like any other patient in ICTU, Susie—we're health professionals, not judges,' Allegra reminded her sternly.

'I know, but what the poor father is being put through…he's a complete wreck,' Susie said. 'And you could hardly blame him for being so angry.'

'Has he been back in?'

'Yes, just a few minutes ago. He didn't stay long. I had to get him a glass of water and a couple of paracetamol almost as soon as he laid eyes on Tommy. I don't think he can handle the sight of his little boy so badly injured. He probably blames himself for not seeing it coming.'

'Yes, I guess you're right,' Allegra agreed with a heavy sigh. 'Suicide always creates such a lot of guilt. You always wonder if you could have done something to prevent it.'

Susie gave her a thoughtful look. 'That sounds to me like the voice of experience. Someone close to you?'

Allegra was privately impressed by the nurse's percipience but didn't know her well enough to share what had happened to her friend Julie during their first year at medical school. She'd only shared it with Louise because Louise's brother had made a suicide attempt a couple of years previously after a relationship break-up. He had recovered, however, and was now in a happy relationship and had dealt with the issues that had led to his attempt on his life.

Allegra's experience with her friend had been a harrowing time and she still had nightmares about it. She still tortured herself over all the signs she'd missed, all the opportunities she could have taken to prevent a tragedy that she knew would haunt her for the rest of her life.

'No…' she answered, straightening the bed clothes over the child. 'But you sort of get to know this stuff from working in a place like this.'

'Yeah, tell me about it,' Susie said. 'You see it all and then have to go home and sleep.'

'Sleep…' Allegra forced a wry smile to her lips. 'Now, there's something that'd be incredibly tempting.'

'Not as tempting as coffee with the new boss,' Susie said with a little twinkle.

Allegra frowned. 'Don't you nurses have anything better to do than gossip all the time? It was just coffee, all right? It doesn't mean a thing.'

'What about Patrick Naylor?'

'What about him?' she snapped back irritably.

'He's not going to be too happy about you fraternising with the director when he had first call.'

'For pity's sake, how often do I have to tell everyone that I am *not* involved with Patrick Naylor?'

'I guess the only way to do that is by making it obvious you're dating someone else,' Susie suggested.

'Yeah—well, maybe I will do just that,' Allegra said, and giving the nurse one last little hardened glare turned on her heel and left.

CHAPTER SIX

JOEL adjusted his tie for the third time and rocked back on his heels as he waited for Allegra to answer her apartment intercom. It had been so long since he'd been on a proper date he'd almost forgotten how to go about it. Not that this was a proper date. Not really. It was dinner with a colleague.

A get-to-know-you-better dinner.

Nothing else.

'Hello?'

'Hi, Allegra, it's me, Joel. Shall I wait for you down here?'

'No, come on up. I'm not quite ready,' she said a little breathlessly.

He made his way to the fifth floor via the lift but before he could raise his hand to knock on her door she opened it and ushered him in.

'Sorry,' she said, stooping to pick an earring off the floor and inserting it in her ear lobe. 'I got held up in traffic. I won't be a minute. Have a seat. Would you like a drink or something?'

'No, I'm fine.'

She gave him a nervous little smile and disappeared into a room that he assumed was her bedroom. He heard a couple of stiff curses as she dropped something and he smiled to himself. Maybe he wasn't the only one who was a little out of practice when it came to dating.

She came out a short time later dressed in a simple black dress with heels that, in spite of their lethal-looking height, still only brought her up to his shoulder. She was wearing subtle make-up, the smoky eye-shadow highlighting her green eyes and sooty dark lashes. Her lips were lightly coated with a pink-tinged gloss and her shoulder-length light brown hair was loose about her shoulders, falling in soft waves that made his fingers itch to reach out and see if it was really as silky as it looked. He had to stuff his hands in his trouser pockets to stop himself from giving in to the temptation.

'I'm sorry to keep you waiting,' she said as she reached for her evening bag on the sofa, sending a soft waft of her light perfume his way. 'I'm not usually so disorganised.'

'It's been a hectic day,' he said. 'I had to rush at the last minute as well.'

Allegra followed him out to his car. 'Do you live close to the hospital?' she asked, once they were on their way.

'I'm just renting a place in South Yarra at the moment,' he answered. 'I'm still trying to work out what sort of place I want to buy.'

'You mean an apartment or a house?'

'Yes. Both have their advantages but with the hours I work it doesn't make sense to rush in and buy a house with a big garden when I haven't even got the time to sit in it, much less maintain it.'

'That's what gardeners are for,' she said. 'I'm even thinking about getting some help in to water my pot plants. I just don't seem to have the time.'

He glanced across at her and smiled. 'You could always get plastic ones.'

'Now, that would really send my mother into a tailspin,' she answered with a dancing gleam in her eyes. 'Fake plants are not good for positive energy flow.'

He turned back to the traffic, a small smile tugging at the corners of his mouth. 'You know something? I'm beginning to suspect you're not quite as alternative as you make out, Allegra Tallis.'

'And you're not quite the overbearing ogre you want everyone to think you are, are you, Joel Addison?'

His warm brown eyes held hers for a moment before shifting away to concentrate on locating a parking spot. 'I guess you'll just have to wait and see.'

The restaurant he'd booked was in Toorak Road and after they were shown to their table and left with menus and the wine list, Allegra felt herself begin to relax a little. She sank into the comfortable chair and examined the menu.

Phew! Not a pizza in sight.

'What's that little smile for?' Joel asked.

She met his gaze across the table. 'I was just checking for pizzas.'

He handed her the wine list. 'Maybe you should choose the red wine. I don't want to be accused of picking a cheap one.'

'You don't strike me as the cheap red wine type,' she said, handing it back to him.

He gave her a teasing look. 'You can tell that from my aura?'

She pursed her mouth at him but ended up releasing it on a reluctant smile. 'I hope you're not trying to pick a fight with me, Dr Addison.'

'Not tonight,' he said. 'We're just too over-worked, tired people having dinner, OK?'

'Now who's reading auras?' she asked. 'And here I was, positive I'd managed to conceal the shadows underneath my eyes.'

'I don't know anything about auras but I can tell you work hard, harder than most.'

'Now, I *am* really going to ask for a refund on that eye cream,' she said with a rueful grimace.

He smiled at her but just then the waiter approached to take their drinks order and to advise them on the daily specials.

Allegra studied Joel covertly as he asked the waiter about the menu, the low, deep timbre of his voice and gentle respectful manner as he listened to the young man telling her more about him as a person than anything else she'd seen so far. She inwardly cringed as she recalled her date with Patrick, who'd practically abused the young inexperienced waitress for not bringing the garlic bread out on time.

After the waiter returned with their wine and took their order for meals, Joel sat back in his seat and surveyed her features in silence for a moment or two.

'So what made you choose coma recovery as a project?' he finally asked.

Allegra met his dark gaze guardedly. 'Is this what

this dinner is about—me having to justify my project to you all over again? If that's the case, I might as well leave now and save the chef the hassle of cooking a meal I won't be able to eat.'

'No, I'm just interested in what motivated you to choose that particular study over any number of other topics you could have chosen instead. There are a lot of people who would feel it's unlikely to produce anything of scientific significance.'

'It's pretty clear which camp you'd be in.'

'Come on, Allegra,' he reasoned. 'Everything in our profession is data-driven now—if you can't measure it, it probably doesn't exist. Anecdotes and expert opinion are no longer good enough.'

She sent him a hardened glare. 'Can we talk about something else?'

'OK, but there are two deeply comatose patients in ICTU right now but I don't want you to do anything that would draw unnecessary attention to the unit at this time.'

'What do you mean by that?' she asked with rising anger. 'What do you think I'm going to do? Cast a spell or something?'

'I just want you to tread very carefully. I'm just concerned that if Mr Lowe's son dies, you could be an easy target to blame.'

'*Me?* What about his wife? She's the one who drove the car!'

'I know, but you know how people are when they're under a lot of stress. The whole spectrum of emotion gets played out in ICU. The very best and worst of human behaviour comes out. In my opinion, Keith Lowe is a litigation time bomb waiting to go off.'

Allegra couldn't help agreeing with him, although it pained her to admit it. 'He does seem the type, I guess,' she said, lowering her gaze a fraction.

'I'm not trying to sabotage your project, Allegra, nothing like that. If anything, I would actually be delighted if you were able to deliver some measurable and repeatable results. But is this the right time to do it, the right case to start with?'

She raised her eyes back to his. 'Are you expressly forbidding me to do anything or just asking me to be discreet?'

He held her gaze for a lengthy period. 'I said I'd give you a month and I'll stick by that. But if you're going to use this case, I want you to keep a low profile. Things are much more tense than usual because of the question mark hanging over Kate Lowe. One press leak and public emotion will be running high. The notion of a mother trying to kill her own child in her own suicide attempt is bizarre—the press would play it from every angle for all it's worth, every day either of them survives. And if, on top of that, they got wind that they were being used in a research project, especially using not-strictly-medical methods, they'd have a field day—none of us might survive it.'

'I understand,' she said. 'But I'd still like to try with the little boy. I'll ask the father for his permission, of course.'

He held her direct look for a moment. 'Fine, but all I'm saying is that emotion runs high when children are involved. Just keep that in mind.'

Allegra thought back to her earlier conversation with Susie but decided against mentioning it. The nursing staff were well used to dealing with all sorts of people and could be relied on to remain professional at all times.

After a short pause she released a heartfelt sigh. 'I often wonder how they get on—you know, once they leave ICU. We patch them up and send them on their way, but we get very little long-term feedback. Don't you wonder how they manage to adjust, especially the ones with permanent disability?'

Joel examined the contents of his wineglass, a

shadow of something coming and going in his dark eyes. 'I try not to think about it too much.'

She looked at him, her expression softening. 'But you do, don't you?'

He gave her a twisted, humourless smile. 'Well, it's part of the job, isn't it? You go home exhausted after long shifts, then you can't sleep, worrying you could have done more.'

'I know… It's a wonder we don't all end up on stress leave.'

'It's why doctors' marriages have a higher than average failure rate,' he said, reaching for his wine and taking a sip.

The waiter arrived with their meals and once he'd left, Allegra said into the little silence that had fallen, 'You never told me what your parents do for a living.'

Joel put his glass back on the table before answering. 'My father is a teacher and my mother hasn't worked outside the home since my brother and I were born.'

'That must have been nice for you and your brother,' she said, 'having a full-time mum at home.'

'It certainly had its advantages.' He reached for his cutlery and asked, 'What about your early childhood? Did your mother choose to work or stay at home?'

'My mother wasn't the stay-at-home type. My father did a lot of the child care in the early days, but I seem to remember a few child-care centres along the way.'

'But you had a happy childhood?'

'Of course. My parents were a bit "out there" at times, but I can't remember ever being unhappy. Even when they went their separate ways, they did it so wonderfully well that I was the envy of all my friends for having such trendy, cool parents.'

Joel looked at her in silent envy. His childhood had been marked with tragedy, a tragedy relentless and ongoing. The last time he'd visited, just two days ago, his mother had aged and visibly shrunk even further, and his father's face had become a mask of pain from their situation, each line more deeply etched, each shadow a darker curtain.

Allegra became aware of his silence and wondered if she was boring him. 'I'm sorry…' She pushed her glass out of her reach. 'I tend to talk too much about myself when I drink wine.'

He gave her a lopsided smile. 'Truth serum?'

'Next I'll be telling you all my innermost secrets.'

'You seem to be pretty much an open book to me. You wear your heart on your sleeve, which is unusual in a medico. It usually gets hammered out of you at medical school.'

She lowered her gaze to the small flickering candle on the table, a small frown bringing her finely arched brows together for a moment. 'Well I must have been absent that day at medical school.'

'What happened?'

Allegra brought her eyes back to his, surprised yet again at the warmth she could see reflected there. 'I lost my best friend during second year.'

'An accident?'

She shook her head. 'Suicide.'

'I'm sorry. That must have been a tough time.'

'It was… I blamed myself for not seeing the signs.'

'Most people who know a suicide victim suffer the same guilt. Look at Mr Lowe today. I'm sure that's why he's unable to cope. He probably thinks it's his fault.'

'Yes…but in Julie's case I should have known. I was her best friend. We'd shared everything since the first day we met during orientation week at university.'

'You can't always read people's minds,' he pointed out.

'My mother would totally disagree with you,' she said, trying to lighten the conversation. She gave him a little smile and added, 'She insists she can infallibly detect what people are thinking just by looking deeply into their eyes.'

'Oh, really?' He didn't bother disguising his scepticism but this time it was tempered with a smile. 'And have you perhaps inherited this little gift?'

'I don't know. I haven't really put it to the test.' She leaned forward to look into his eyes. 'Let me see now… Hmm—you definitely have sleep on your mind. I can see you haven't had a decent night's sleep in weeks if not months.'

'Not bad,' he said. 'There might be something in this after all.'

She leaned closer to peer even more, her hair falling forward to brush the back of his hand where it rested on the table near his glass in a soft-as-air caress that sent a charge of electricity straight to his groin as her greener-than-green gaze meshed with his.

'What do you see in my eyes now?' he asked, his voice sounding a little rough around the edges.

Allegra looked deeply into his darker-than-night eyes, an unexpected pulse of desire beginning to beat a steady tattoo low and deep in her body. Her chest felt as if it had shrunk to half its size, the air she tried to breathe into her lungs catching on its way down. She moistened her lips, her skin lifting in awareness in a way that had never happened to her before. Her breasts felt full and heavy, her nipples puckering beneath her black lace bra as she felt the searing burn of his dark gaze as it held hers.

She sat back in her chair and tucked her hair behind her ear as she gave a little self-conscious laugh. 'I've definitely had way too much wine to drink.'

'The eyes are supposed to be the window to the soul,' he said as he signalled to the waiter for the bill. 'But what if you don't have one?'

'Everyone has a soul,' she protested.

He gave her one of his cynical smiles. 'Don't go looking for one in me, Allegra, for you won't find one. It died a long time ago.'

Allegra followed him out of the restaurant a short time later, her heart contracting painfully at the thought of what he had seen and experienced out in the field to have hardened him in such a way. She'd seen shadows of pain in his eyes that she knew no amount of sleep would ever erase. And she knew if he'd looked deeply into her own he would have found the very same shadows lurking there…

CHAPTER SEVEN

'THANK you for dinner,' Allegra said once he'd walked her to the door of her apartment block. 'I had a good time. It was a nice restaurant. Not a pizza in sight.'

'Aren't you going to ask me in for coffee?'

'I was going to but I wasn't sure if you would take it the wrong way.'

'I take it the same way you do—black.'

She gave him a quelling look. 'I meant...well, you know what I meant.'

He smiled at her flustered expression and before he could stop himself lifted a finger to her cheek, trailing his knuckle over the creamy curve where a spot of heightened colour had pooled.

Allegra ran her tongue over her lips in a nervous gesture. 'I'd better go in. It's getting late and I'm on early and...' She stopped when she saw the dark glitter in his eyes as they caught and held hers, her stomach hollowing in anticipation.

His head came down slowly, his warm breath brushing over her lips before he placed his mouth on hers in a soft, hardly touching kiss.

She looked up at him, her heart increasing its pace as he ran his tongue over his lips as if tasting her sweetness.

'I probably shouldn't have done that,' he said.

She swallowed the restriction in her throat and croaked, 'Why?'

'Because now I know what it feels like, I want to do it again.'

'Oh…'

'It could cause all sorts of problems,' he said, taking her by the shoulders and bringing her one tiny step closer, her breasts brushing against his chest.

'You think so?' she asked, leaning into his hardness instinctively.

'I know so.'

'Too bad…'

He held her gaze for several pulsing seconds. 'The gossip would be unbearable.'

'Totally…'

'And then there's the problem of shifts.'

'Yes...' She moistened her lips again. 'That's always a downside.'

'And then there's the issue of your place or mine.'

'Tricky.'

He smiled and tipped up her chin. 'You are one hell of a temptation, Allegra Tallis, but I'm going to be the strong one here and step back before we drift into dangerous territory.'

'OK...' She swallowed again as she felt the hard ridge of his growing erection against her. 'That would be wise, I guess.'

'Very wise.'

A full thirty seconds passed.

'So...so why aren't you doing it?' she asked.

'Doing what?'

'Stepping back,' she said. 'You said you were going to be the strong one and step back.'

'You're right,' he said, his gaze dipping to her mouth. 'Now would be a good time.'

'A very good time...'

Her stomach did a complete somersault as his hands slid down the length of her bare arms to encircle her wrists.

'Why don't we do it on the count of three?' he suggested, after another heart-stopping pause.

Allegra's fingers curled around the length and

strength of his. 'Right…let's do that. On the count of three.' She took a breath and began the countdown, 'One…'

'Two…' he said, and released her wrists to place his hands on her hips.

Another deep throb of silence passed. Allegra knew it was her turn to say the last number but somehow she couldn't get the one word past the trembling shield of her lips. Her gaze locked with his as the time beat on, his hands on her hips feeling like a slow burn as his heat passed from his body to hers.

'Aren't you going to say it?' he asked, his breath caressing the surface of her mouth as his head came inexorably closer.

'I was getting to it…'

She felt the imprint of his lazy smile on her lips before he gradually increased the pressure, each slow drugging movement of his mouth on hers sending her senses into overload. The sexual charge of his tongue probing for entry made her legs buckle with instant uncontrollable need and she pressed herself against him, relishing in the feel of his body's instant reaction to hers. She wasn't without experience but never had she felt the energy and force of such fierce attraction before.

It was like her body had been storing up its need for this moment when his mouth scorched its timeless message on hers.

Her tongue played with his boldly, each movement inciting her desire to a higher level, moving even further out of her control. Her mind swam with images of how they would be together, his strong leanly muscled body pinning her beneath him.

A passing car's headlights brought her back to earth with a shaft of exposing light that she knew would do her no credit with her overly conservative neighbours.

She eased her mouth away from his and said somewhat breathlessly, 'Th-three.'

Joel's hands moved from her hips, his wry smile sending another wave of longing through her. 'There, I knew you could do it.'

'It was a tough call but I guess someone has to do it.'

'Yes,' he said, brushing the curve of her cheek once more. 'Someone does.'

'So...' She tried to sound casually unaffected, as if she kissed handsome, full-blooded men on her doorstep all the time. 'I guess I'll see you at work tomorrow.'

'Yes, I guess you will.'

''Night…'

'Goodnight, Allegra. I really enjoyed this evening. You're surprisingly good company.'

'Better than an internet date?'

'Way better,' he said, staring again at her mouth.

'Um…this is the bit where you go down those steps and get in your car and drive home,' she said, pointing to where his car was. 'Do you think you can manage that?'

'I'm working myself up to it.'

She couldn't help laughing. 'You have definitely graduated with honours from the school of irresistible charm.'

He bent his head and pressed a soft kiss to the side of her mouth. 'So have you, Dr Tallis.' He gave her cheek one last gentle flick with his finger and stepped away, walking with long strides towards his car.

'Have a good sleep,' she called out, as he got in his car.

He turned his head to lock gazes with her. 'Are you joking?'

'No…not really…'

He lifted his hand in a wave and with a deep throaty roar of the engine drove off and disappeared around the corner.

* * *

Joel hadn't expected to sleep but when the phone rang beside his bed at three a.m. he realised he'd been in a deep dreamless slumber that took some effort on his part to come out of. He reached blindly for the phone and answered it groggily, 'Joel Addison.'

'Dr Addison, it's Brian Willis, I'm on night shift for the unit. We've got one hell of a problem here. I thought I should tell you about it now instead of when you come in the morning.'

Joel rubbed his face and sat up. 'What problem? What's going on?'

'It's Mrs Lowe,' Brian said. 'Her ventilator has been tampered with and she had a respiratory arrest.'

'*What?*' Joel leapt off the bed, his pulse accelerating. 'What the hell do you mean, her ventilator was interfered with? Interfered with by whom? Is she all right?'

'She's fine, Dr Addison. It's all back under control here, but the nursing staff are very shaken. Judy Newlands was looking after her and raised the alarm. If she wasn't as organised and level-headed as she is, it could have been a total disaster,' Brian said. 'Someone had switched off the ventilator alarms and switched oxygen and nitrous oxide inputs to the ventilator—she was breathing a 50-50 mix of nitrous and air.'

'That's impossible, Brian, the connectors are different. You can't screw an oxygen supply to a nitrous inlet, or vice versa.'

'I know that, but that's not how they did it. They cut the tubing and used clip-on joiners to switch the tubing. Nitrous comes out of the wall, and halfway along the tubing it changes into the oxygen tubing input of the ventilator. And the opposite for the oxygen supply.'

'This is serious, Brian. I'll be there in fifteen minutes. Have hospital security and the police been notified?'

'The place is crawling with them right now, Dr Addison, and somehow the press has been informed. There are at least two newspapers here already and security tells me there's a TV news van setting up a satellite dish out the front.'

Joel let out one sharp expletive. 'I'll be there as soon as I can.'

A group of journalists approached Joel as soon as he headed for the front doors of the unit. 'Dr Addison? You're the new director of Melbourne Memorial's innovative new ICTU. Do you have any comments on Kate or Tommy Lowe's condition? Has this incident or accident in the unit involved either of them?' one of them fired at him.

'I'm sorry but I am not at liberty to discuss patient details with anyone other than close family members,' he said, and made to brush past.

'Dr Addison, there are rumours that Kate Lowe tried to kill herself and her son, and there are rumours that an attempt was made on her life in the early hours of this morning in your unit. Do you believe there is a major weakness in security in the new unit? Could anyone just walk in and interfere with patients?'

'Is the public safe in your unit, Dr Addison?' another journalist persisted.

'Please, get out of my way,' Joel said, swiping his pass key to enter the building.

He located Brian Willis and almost frog-marched him into his office. Once there, the door shutting behind them with a snap, he asked Brian to fill him in on events of the night in detail.

'Whoever did this didn't realise about all the other separate alarms,' Brian said. 'The first thing to go off was the alarm on the pulse oximeter. Then the heartrate alarm went off at the desk. We were a bit short on staff, and had a one-to-three nursing ratio for about fifteen minutes down that end of the unit. Judy had gone to mix an antibiotic dose for Tommy, I was in the office. Judy heard the first alarm and came back in. The ventilator seemed to be working fine, she saw the alarms were off and switched them back on, and of course they all started sounding off. Oxygen sats had dropped to 70 per cent, so Judy just disconnected Mrs Lowe from the ventilator and hand-bagged her. Her obs came back to normal. She then reset all the ventilator settings and reconnected her, but within a minute all the alarms went off again.

We decided the ventilator was faulty. We bagged her while one of the unused machines was brought across by Chris Farmer, the orderly. We set her up on it on its bottle supply and it worked fine, so we disconnected the wall supply, moved out the old one, moved in the new one, connected the wall supply to the new one, then all the alarms went off on the new one. We knew the wall supply must have been OK because it's driving every other ventilator in the unit. It's just didn't add up. Then Chris found the connectors and switched-over tubing—one loop of it, with the connectors, was concealed under the equipment trolley in the corner of the cubicle.'

'This is not just sabotage, Brian, this is attempted murder,' Joel said.

'I agree. The police think so, too. They're interviewing Judy and Chris now. I gave a statement a while ago. They want to talk to you at some point.'

'Were there any relatives in the unit?'

'There were people coming and going earlier in the night, up till pretty late actually,' Brian answered. 'You know what it's like in here sometimes, we allow relatives as much contact as possible. That boy that came in the other day—you know, the spinal injury? His parents have barely left his bedside. I think his sister and girlfriend have been in, too, but it's impossible to keep track of everybody in a unit as big as this.'

Joel ran a distracted hand through his hair. 'I know…it's hard to tell people to stay away when it could be the last time they see the patient.' His hand fell to his side. 'Has Mrs Lowe's husband been informed?'

'Yes.'

'What was his reaction?'

'Apparently pretty cold and dismissive about it,' Brian said. 'Quite frankly, I don't think he'd care if someone pulled the plug on his wife.'

Joel frowned. 'Was he in the unit at any time during the night?'

'I'm not sure, I'd have to check with the nursing staff. Do you think he did this?'

'It'd be a pretty stupid thing to do under the circumstances,' Joel said. 'The finger of blame would point straight at him.'

'Yeah, I guess you're right. But he must be extremely cheesed off about it all the same. The kid isn't doing so well. Mr Lowe will probably lose it if his son doesn't recover or if he's left permanently brain-damaged.'

'Let's hope it doesn't turn out to be permanent,' Joel said, at the same time as his phone rang.

'I'll leave you to it,' Brian said and made his way out.

'Joel, it's Patrick Naylor here,' said the voice on the phone. 'What the hell is going on in the unit? I just had a call from Switchboard that the press and the police are crawling all over the place.'

'There's been an incident in ICTU with a patient,' Joel explained, pinching the bridge of his nose with two fingers to release the tension he could feel building behind his eyes. 'It's under control now but the press will expect a statement from one of us—if it's me, I want you to clear it before I make it. You'd better come in and I'll fill you in with the details.'

'For God's sake, man, it's four a.m.!' the CEO said. 'Can't it wait until morning? I normally don't get in till eight-thirty.'

Joel dropped his hand and rolled his eyes, actively forcing himself to remain polite. 'If that's what you'd prefer.'

'Good. I'll see you in my office at eight-thirty. And get Security to get rid of the press. I don't want to be harassed by journalists getting from my car to the lifts.'

'Fine, but if it's going to be eight-thirty I can't be held responsible for whatever unenlightened speculation appears on the front of the Melbourne papers,' Joel said, but the CEO had already hung up.

CHAPTER EIGHT

'DID you hear what happened last night in ICTU?' Margaret Hoffman, the anaesthetic registrar, said the next morning as she came into the main operating theatre change room where Allegra was changing for the first case on Harry Upton's long list.

'No, I came straight up here. I'm doing my round later. What happened?'

'Someone tried to kill Kate Lowe.'

'What?' Allegra's eyes went wide. 'How?'

'They tampered with the ventilator, cut and switched nitrous and oxygen gas lines into her ventilator.'

'That's incredible! Have they caught the person responsible?'

'No, but I bet it was the father,' Margaret said.

'It could have been anyone,' Allegra said, not sure why she was springing to Keith Lowe's defence. 'It might have even been a member of staff.'

Margaret frowned as she tightened the waist ties on her scrub trousers. 'But if it was a staff member, they would have known how the alarm system worked and circumvented it. That woman would be dead by now and I know a few people who would be glad of it.'

'Come on, Margaret, that's a bit harsh, isn't it? The police haven't even established whether it was an attempted murder-suicide.'

Margaret handed her the newspaper from inside her locker. 'Haven't you read this morning's paper?'

Allegra unfolded it and looked down at the front-page story, her stomach sinking in alarm. There was a fairly recent picture of Kate and Tommy and below, the stark black headlines couldn't have been more condemning of the mother's motives.

'She's as guilty as all get-out,' Margaret said. 'Look at her. She looks the type, all dowdy and depressed. The inside story is the husband asked for a divorce and it sent her crazy. She didn't want to give up custody of the little boy so decided to take matters into her own hands.'

Allegra refolded the paper and handed it back. 'She's still entitled to a fair trial.'

'Yeah, right, where she gets some hot-shot lawyer to get her to plead temporary insanity and she gets off scot-free,' Margaret said in a scathing tone. 'What's fair about that? How does that help that poor little kid hooked up on that ventilator?'

'What would help both Tommy and his mother would be the staff getting on with their job of taking care of their recovery instead of gossiping and speculating about them,' Allegra said.

'Surely you don't think she's innocent, do you?' Margaret asked. 'How can she be when she was high on drugs and drink? She was driving the car, remember, no one else.'

'I know…' Allegra sighed as she stepped out of her skirt. 'But I just can't get my head around the idea of someone trying to kill their own child, not unless they were actually not in their right mind.'

'I feel sorry for the husband,' Margaret said. 'It said in the paper how he'd done everything he could to try and save the marriage.'

Allegra frowned as she tied her hair with a bandana. 'And yet the paper said he asked for a divorce.'

'Well, everyone has their limits,' Margaret said. 'Maybe he'd finally had enough and found someone else. That's the trend, isn't it? Trade in the old wife for an updated version?'

Allegra turned to face her, a contemplative expression beginning to settle on her features. 'Or get *rid* of the old wife.'

Margaret's mouth dropped open. 'But how would he have done it? When it happened he was in Melbourne. He's got an iron-clad alibi.' She folded her arms across her chest and added, 'Now who is doing the speculating?'

'You're right,' Allegra said with a rueful twist to her mouth. 'We'd better leave this stuff to the professionals while we get on with what we're trained to do. Is Harry here yet? I want to get on with the list so I can do some preliminary work on Tommy and his mother.'

'So you've managed to convince the new director, have you?'

'I wouldn't go as far as using the word "convince",' Allegra said. 'He has a lot of reservations. And this latest drama is not going to help things. Everyone will be as edgy as all get-out around there. But unless Kate or Tommy wake up, we're never going to know what happened—the truth might never come out. Maybe a murderer will walk free. As I see it, my project is now doubly important.'

'But what if the truth is she did try to kill her son and herself? How is the little boy going to cope with that?'

Allegra sighed as she reached for her theatre clogs. 'How does anyone cope with the truth? It hurts for a while but somehow you have to pick yourself up and get on with life. Kids are amazingly resilient and incredibly forgiving.'

'I can tell you one thing for free—if that woman was my mother, I would never forgive her,' Margaret said with feeling. 'That kid is likely to be brain-damaged for the rest of his life. That's beyond forgiveness, if you ask me.'

'No one is beyond forgiveness, Margaret. There isn't a person alive who hasn't made a mistake some time during their lives. We don't know the circumstances of Kate Lowe's life, or at least not firsthand. She might have felt completely different on another day. That's the hardest part of it to comprehend. What loomed so large in her life might have been dealt with totally differently, given a few hours either way. And as for Tommy, well, at this stage we don't know the extent of his brain injury,' Allegra reminded her. 'For all we know, he could make a complete and full recovery.'

Margaret gave her a sceptical look as she shouldered open the change-room door. 'You really do believe in miracles, don't you?'

'We have to sometimes, Margaret,' she said. 'Science can't fix some things, and it can't tell us our values. If we haven't got values, we may as well go downstairs and turn off the ventilator now.'

'God, I hope it doesn't ever come to turning off Tommy's ventilator.' Margaret grimaced. 'Especially not so soon after Alice Greeson.'

'It won't come to that, Margaret,' Allegra said with determination. 'I'm going to do everything in my power to make sure of it.'

Allegra had not long finished Harry's list, which had run overtime due to a complication with a patient, when she received a call from the CEO, insisting on an immediate meeting with him in his office. 'But I have to get down to ICTU,' she said, hoping to put him off.

'Why?' Patrick's tone became resentful. 'So you can have a little rendezvous with the new director? I heard about your cosy little dinner last night.'

Allegra felt her hackles rising. 'Look, Patrick, I'm sorry but I'm not interested in a relationship with you. What I do in my spare time is my business. I'm sorry to be so blunt, but that's the way it is.'

There was a tense little silence.

'It's all right, I understand, but can't we just meet as friends?' Patrick asked, his tone now sounding more than a little emotional. 'You've been wonderful to me lately, that's why I supported your project so strenuously, apart from the fact that I do think it has merit. I felt I owed it to you for being such a good friend to me when I most needed it. Meet for a drink tonight at the Elgin Street bar at seven-thirty. That's all I'm asking. Please, Allegra.'

Allegra suppressed a sigh of resignation. Patrick was right. He had gone out on a limb for her and she owed him her friendship at the very least. 'All right, just one drink. But as friends, nothing else,' she relented.

'That's fine,' Patrick said. 'But I still thought I should warn you about getting involved with the new director. You'll only get hurt.'

She felt her tension increase slightly. There was a hint of something in the CEO's tone that made her blood feel a little cold in her veins. 'What are you saying, Patrick?' she asked.

'Look, I know he's a damn good intensivist but I can tell you right now he only asked you out last night to keep you away from the unit. He doesn't want you messing with the Lowe boy.'

'Come on, Patrick, that's an outright lie,' she said, but the black, long-legged spider of doubt was already crawling insidiously across her mind as she recalled Joel's totally-out-of-the-blue dinner invitation. They had barely been seated at the table when he'd brought up the topic of her study and the dangers of involving Kate and Tommy Lowe in it.

'Go and ask him,' Patrick challenged her. 'He won't deny it. He doesn't want you to interfere with how the unit is being run. The press attention has been damaging enough. They're making the unit sound as if anyone can walk in on any patient in there. And if they get to hear of you waving crystals or scented candles about, we'll be a laughing stock.'

'But you said—'

'I know what I said and I still stand by it. I do think your project has potential but I'm afraid I'm with Joel Addison on this particular case. There's just too much at stake. Just keep that in mind if he asks you out again. He could be operating under false pretences.'

'Don't worry, I will,' she said, and after a quick goodbye stuffed the phone back in her pocket.

Joel was returning to his office after the X-ray review meeting in the radiology department when he encountered Allegra stalking up the corridor towards him, her face looking like a brewing storm.

'Just the person I was hoping to run into,' he

said with a smile. 'Got time for a quick coffee in my office?'

Allegra gritted her teeth. 'Why? So you can keep me out of the unit and away from my project for a little longer?'

He frowned at her tone. 'What's that supposed to mean?'

'Surely you don't need me to spell out your own despicable motives for you.'

'I haven't the faintest idea of what you're talking about.'

She gave him a glowering look. 'Why did you ask me out for dinner last night?'

He met her glittering green gaze head on. 'Why does any man ask a beautiful woman out for a meal?'

Allegra had to force herself not to be mollified by his compliment and injected even more venom into her tone. 'If you were any other man, I would have answered that you wanted to get to know me, but I am well aware of your real reasons for taking me out.'

'All right,' he said with a crooked smile. 'I admit it. I had an ulterior motive.'

There was a three-beat pause.

'Well,' she said with a dark frown, 'aren't you going to come clean?'

He took her by the hand before she could stop him and pulled her into a storeroom off the corridor and closed the door. She opened her mouth to rail at him but his mouth came swooping down and covered hers with a hot drugging kiss that left her breathless and totally disorientated in the dark, suddenly intimate confines of the small room. His body was pressed so tightly against hers she could feel the small buttons on his shirt through the thin cotton of her top and his belt buckle against her stomach. She had trouble containing her reaction to him. It seemed to come from deep inside, out of reach of her brain, which insisted she remove herself from his embrace.

He lifted his mouth from hers and flicked on the light switch near her left shoulder, his dark eyes smouldering with desire as he held her gaze.

'You had no right to do that,' she said, wishing her voice had sounded a little more strident and infuriated, instead of breathless and weak.

'You asked me to explain my motives. I thought it best to demonstrate them instead.'

'What you just demonstrated is your incredible gall. You only asked me out last night to lure me away from the unit so don't bother denying it.'

'I'm not going to deny it.'

She glared at him furiously. 'How dare you pretend to be attracted to me? That is so low.'

'I'm not pretending anything, Allegra.'

'I don't believe you,' she tossed back. 'You've been against me from the start. I should have guessed you were up to something when you dropped that dinner invitation into the conversation so unexpectedly.'

'I admit it was a little spontaneous but—'

'Spontaneous?' She felt like stamping her foot in fury. 'You deliberately lured me away from the unit.'

'I asked you out to dinner, for God's sake.' His voice began to tighten in anger. 'Is there a law against that these days? What is it with you? I asked you out because I'm attracted to you and I want to get to know you, but if you're not interested, fine. Maybe I'll take my chances with that internet dating thing after all.'

'I hope you end up with a psychopathic crackpot,' she returned bitterly.

'Yeah, well, it wouldn't be the first time,' he said, and, brushing past her, clicked the door shut behind him.

ICTU was quieter than normal due to the high level of security. Relatives of patients were being asked to limit their visits and to submit to a bag search, and the staff also had to comply with security measures—bag and locker searches, and a permanent security guard in the unit.

Kate had now been moved into one of the isolation rooms and was under police guard. Tommy was still showing no signs of waking, and the nurse on duty for him, Bethany Gladstone, relayed the neurosurgical plan for a repeat brain CT and an EEG.

'Has the father been in today?' Allegra asked.

'He's been in and out,' Bethany said. 'He should be back any time. He was going to have a bite to eat.'

Allegra looked at the unconscious child on the bed and wondered how anyone could think of food when their only child was hovering precariously between life and death.

'He's a bit of a detached sort of bloke, don't you think?' Bethany said. 'The father, I mean.'

'Why do you say that?'

The nurse gave a little shrug. 'I don't know... He just doesn't seem to be all that keen on hanging around here.'

'It's tough on parents,' Allegra said. 'They don't always cope with the emotions of it all. It doesn't get much worse than this—the thought of losing your only child.'

'Yeah, I guess so,' Bethany said. 'What's your plan with him?'

'Tommy, you mean?'

Bethany nodded.

Allegra looked at the little boy for a moment. 'I'd like to speak to the father about Tommy's history. The things he loves—books, movies, that sort of thing. I want to feel as if I know him in order to find ways to get through to him.'

'His father doesn't seem the type who knows his son all that well. Some dads are very hands on, sitting and talking to their kids, holding their hands, stroking them and so on. I don't think Mr Lowe has touched his son once the whole time I've been on duty.'

'Not all fathers are the same,' Allegra said. 'Besides, you know how some people can't cope with illness and the prospect of death. They come in here and totally freak out when they see all the machines, while others react with calm.'

'Yeah, well, I think Mr Lowe needs to take lessons on fatherhood from Jonathon Sprent's father. Ever since that young man has been in here with that spinal injury his dad has hardly left the bedside, neither has his mum. That's what I call perfect parenting.'

'How is he doing? I haven't had much to do with his case.'

'Anthony Pardle did a spinal decompression and things are looking a little more hopeful—he's had a tingling sensation in his legs.'

'That's good. Even after all this training and time, I still can't bear the thought of a young man of nineteen confined to a wheelchair for the rest of his life,' Allegra said.

'I know,' Bethany sighed. 'He's had some time off the ventilator and coped pretty well. There's talk of moving him to the high-dependency unit in a couple of days.'

'It's nice to hear of something positive happening around here,' she said, looking at Tommy again.

'So you want me to let you know when Mr Lowe gets back?' Bethany asked.

'That would be great, thanks,' Allegra said, turning around to face her again. 'I'll be in the ICTU office, catching up on paperwork.'

A short time later Allegra looked up to see Keith Lowe outside the glassed-in office in ICTU. She got to her feet and with a reassuring smile led him to a private corner so she could speak to him.

'How are you doing, Mr Lowe?'

'I'm fine, but I want to know what's happening with my son,' he said rather impatiently. 'I've got a business to run and all this waiting about is not helping.'

Allegra had to fight down her instinctive reaction to his callous dismissal of his son's condition in preference to his career. 'Tommy is doing as well as can be expected at this stage,' she said.

'Look, Dr…er, Tallis,' he said, peering at her name badge. 'I want my son out of here, and fast. Don't get me wrong. My business can wait, but I can't juggle the two like this for too much longer. Is there anything I can do to help my son regain consciousness?'

'Yes, there is, actually,' she said, hope lifting like a suddenly inflated balloon in her chest. 'I need you to tell me some of Tommy's favourite things at present, such as music, stories he likes to hear or read, movies or DVDs he likes to watch, activities.'

'That's easy,' Keith said. 'Tommy has been totally obsessed with the Harry Potter stories. Whenever I get the chance, I read him his favourite passages. I bought him the first DVD and he's watched it countless times. He can even recite the dialogue practically verbatim.'

'Brilliant!' Allegra said. 'Would you have any objection to me setting up a portable DVD player near him to see if it triggers brain activity?'

He frowned at her. 'You think playing a DVD will make him regain consciousness?'

'I'm not making any promises but the human brain is complicated. Sometimes neural activity can stop for functional reasons when there is no physical damage. Tommy's brain CT looks normal. CTs are not perfect—there could be widespread scattered damage that doesn't show up on CT and could be enough to be severe brain damage. But the normal CT could alternatively give us hope. It is possible that there are functional blocks to Tommy's brain activity. It might be feasible to kick-start his conscious processes. The five senses—touch, smell, taste, sight and hearing—if we could find some powerful stimuli through one or two of these that trigger potent memories—that could trigger consciousness. Perhaps listening to his favourite movie will trigger something in Tommy's subconscious and he will start to wake up. There's no guarantee, and not a lot of research in this area—but with someone like Tommy it's worth trialling the technique.'

'If you think there's a chance...' Keith didn't sound particularly optimistic but Allegra refused to be daunted. She'd already passed the biggest hurdle: parental permission.

'I'll organise everything,' she said. 'I have a

portable DVD player and I even have my own copy
of the movie. Is there anything else you can think
of that Tommy particularly likes? Songs he always
listens to, favourite foods?'

Keith wrinkled his nose in scepticism. 'What, are
you going to wave chicken nuggets and chips
under his nose to see if he responds?'

'Is that his favourite food?'

The set of his shoulders seemed to go down a
notch as he let out a deep sigh. 'So often I'd come
home and…Kate would have no dinner prepared.'
He looked at her and continued, 'Don't misunderstand me. I'm not really the where's-my-dinner
type, but Tommy's a little kid—he needs regular
meals. My wife wasn't good at doing that stuff and
because of the pressures of my job I'm away a lot.
I can't remember the last time she actually cooked
a real meal—one that didn't come out of a packet
with instructions to heat and serve.'

'It's not easy, being a mother,' Allegra felt compelled to put in, given her own shortcomings when
it came to preparing gourmet meals. 'There's so
much to do and so little time to do it, especially
with a small child underfoot.'

'I know…' He gave her a vestige of a smile but
there was no humour in it. 'Have you got kids?'

'Er…no…'

'It all changes once you do, you know,' he said. 'You have such ideals, but when reality hits they come crashing down.'

'This is a hard time for you, Mr Lowe. But I think we can work together to try to get Tommy to wake up, if it's at all possible. You love him and even though you might not think he is aware of your presence here, it's definitely possible that in some way he is conscious of it. He's just not quite able to wake up.'

'When will he be able to?'

She touched him gently on the arm. 'I hope he will wake up when we touch on what's most important to him. It could be the movie. Maybe it could be your voice or your touch. If we can just find the trigger that will get him to respond.'

'Have you done this sort of thing before?' he asked. 'You know…woken someone from a deep coma?'

Allegra pushed Alice Greeson's broken body from her mind and tried to concentrate on the rare successes she'd had so far. 'I have had some success, yes.'

'What about my wife?' he asked, his tone becoming harsh. 'Are you going to try and coax her awake as well?'

'I would like Kate to regain consciousness so we could at the very least establish what actually happened and why,' she said.

His eyes became like chips of cold blue ice. 'What happened was she wanted to take Tommy away from me permanently.'

'So there's absolutely no doubt in your mind that Kate tried to take her own life and that of Tommy?'

'Of course there's no doubt. It's what the police suspected from the start. She tried to commit suicide and kill Tommy to get back at me for asking for a divorce.'

'When did you ask her for a divorce?' Allegra asked, watching him closely.

He gave a shrug, his eyes falling away from hers. 'I don't know…a couple of days ago.'

'What was her immediate reaction to your request?'

'She wasn't too happy about it, obviously.'

'Did she say or do anything then to make you suspect she would take things this far?'

His eyes came back to hers, his expression growing impatient. 'Look, Dr Tallis, I have no idea what was going on in my wife's mind. Quite frankly, I haven't for years. I just wanted to end the marriage as soon as possible. I gave it my best shot but I decided it was time to leave.'

'Did you discuss custodial arrangements with Kate when you asked for a divorce?'

'I might have. I don't really remember. Now, if you'll excuse me, I have to get back to the office. I have a meeting and I'm already twenty minutes late as it is.'

Allegra watched him walk out briskly, as if he couldn't wait to get out of the building. He didn't even pause by his son's bed on the way past.

'What did I tell you?' Bethany said, joining her once more. 'Cold and clinical.'

'He certainly is,' Allegra agreed. 'But at least he's given me the go-ahead to work with Tommy. I was worried he might dismiss it right out of hand, but he was surprisingly agreeable.'

'I don't suppose he wants you to work on his wife,' Bethany said cynically.

'No, but that doesn't mean I can't.' Allegra looked towards the isolation room where Kate was being monitored, a tiny frown bringing her brows together. 'Has anyone been in to see her yet?'

'No one at all. I guess she either doesn't have any relatives or if she does, they're all too angry with her to visit—not that you could blame them after what she tried to do.'

'Surely there must be someone close to her, a

friend or sister or cousin, if not her parents. She can't possibly be all alone in the world. Someone must care about her.'

'Doesn't look like it,' Bethany said, 'Unless the husband has deliberately not told them.'

'It's been in the papers though…'

'Not everyone reads the paper every day,' Bethany said.

'True, but news has a habit of travelling anyhow so you'd think someone would have at least called to ask after her by now.'

'I guess you're right,' Bethany said. 'And when you think about it, Tommy hasn't had too many visitors either.'

'Has anyone apart from his father been in?'

'Mr Lowe's sister, Tommy's aunt, has come in a couple of times.'

'What was she like?'

Bethany screwed up her face. 'Exactly like her brother, cold and distant. She was dressed to the nines—you know the type, the cloying perfume and the coiffed hair and designer gear and heavy jewellery. She barely sat by Tommy's bed for more than a minute or two before leaving.'

'Does Tommy have grandparents?'

'I heard one of the nurses ask Mr Lowe that

earlier,' Bethany said. 'He made no mention of Kate's parents but he said his were travelling some-where interstate and couldn't be contacted.'

Allegra's frown increased. 'Which probably means he doesn't want them to be contacted. I wonder why?'

'Beats me,' Bethany said. Changing the subject, she asked, 'What are you going to do with Tommy?'

'His father said he loves Harry Potter movies. I'd like to set one up playing next to his bed—it might trigger memories, stir some neurological activity. It's part of the coma recovery protocol, using familiar auditory stimuli as triggers.'

'What are you going to play it on? This place is pretty cluttered as it is.'

'I've got a portable DVD player and stereo ear-pieces,' Allegra said as she reached for a piece of equipment. 'I'll set it up on the side shelf out of the way. Also, I want to put on a BIS monitor to record any sort of cerebral activity. This strip sticks on his forehead, and the lead plugs into the monitor. This one's got an eight-hour recorder. I'll set it going now, and take a baseline record. In an hour, can you plug in the earpieces and start the DVD? When it's finished, just take out the earpieces. Leave the BIS going till I come in later tonight, OK?'

'Sure' said Bethany. 'Got that. What time will you be back in?'

'About eight-thirty tonight, I think. I've just got one social engagement, and then I'll come in and collect the stuff and go home.'

'I didn't know you even had a home,' Bethany said with a wry grin. 'You seem to spend most of your time here.'

Allegra sent her a rolled eyed look as she left. 'Don't remind me.'

CHAPTER NINE

ALLEGRA had not long completed the pre-admission clinic for Harry Upton's list for the following week when her mobile phone buzzed with an incoming text. She looked down at it and saw it was from Tony Ringer, the night duty intensivist, informing her that Joel was in the high-dependency unit with Harry Upton, assessing the patient who'd had the complication after surgery that morning and that Joel needed anaesthetic information urgently.

Allegra remembered the case well. Gaile Donovan was a forty-eight-year-old woman with ovarian cancer that had invaded the pelvic wall and sigmoid colon. Harry had helped the gynaecologist with the pelvic exploration. The gynaecologist had been keen to get the tumour out but after five litres of blood loss, the normally calm-under-pressure Harry had broken out in a sweat trying to control the bleeding and had insisted they pull the plug before the patient expired on the table. They had packed the pelvis and temporarily closed the abdomen, with the intention of a second-look laparotomy the next day.

When Allegra arrived in HDU, she could hear Harry and Joel discussing the plan of action.

'The patient's BP has hit the floor, Harry,' Joel said. 'She's obviously bleeding again—you have no choice but to operate again now.'

'It was a nightmare the first time around,' Harry said. 'I think an angiogram and embolisation would be a better choice for controlling the bleeding.'

'Listen, Harry,' Joel said. 'She's pouring blood and wouldn't survive the trip to X-Ray, let alone a couple of hours on the X-ray table, having films done. The blood loss has got to be stopped or at least slowed a hell of a lot first. Maybe embolisation, then.'

'Damn it! I wish I'd never become involved in this case,' Harry grumbled. 'I could see it was trouble as soon as we opened.'

'Use the theatre here,' Joel suggested. 'It's on site, it's staffed and it's got angiography capability. Why don't you talk to Radiology now so they come in and set up in case you want to do on-table embolisation?' He turned as he saw Allegra, his expression visibly hardening. 'I thought Tony called for the anaesthetist on duty.'

'I'm the one he called, but if you'd prefer someone else, fine—go ahead,' she said with a flash of her green eyes.

He shifted his mouth in what was clearly reluctant resignation and turned back to Harry. 'Dr Tallis can anaesthetise for you. I've got to get a new central line in quickly to catch up with volume.'

'Right.' Harry nodded in agreement and with a quick grimace in Allegra's direction headed towards Radiology and the ICTU theatre.

Once Harry had left, Joel turned to fill Allegra in on the patient's condition. 'Mrs Donovan's MAP's 50, pulse 160, sats 80—not good. I've got a norad infusion up and fresh blood pouring in, but she needs surgical control of the bleeding. I'm replacing your central line from this morning—it seems to be kinked or compressed somewhere and I just can't get enough volume through it. Harry's using the theatre here.'

Allegra had to force aside her personal issues with him to maintain professional calm. 'I'll head down now and set up. Will you bring her down?'

'Yes, in about ten minutes. How much blood altogether did she have in Theatre this morning? I haven't had time to familiarise myself with the anaesthetic charts here—it would take me ten minutes to add it all up.'

'Yes, they are confusing. Fifteen units of packed cells and four units of whole blood. She also had four packs of albumin volume expander and three fresh-frozen plasmas. How many have you crossed-matched now?'

'Twenty packed cells—that's the current hospital supply of B at the moment. Red Cross are bleeding call-ins tonight to replenish supplies,' he answered.

'Good. I'd better get going,' Allegra said, and left the unit.

Joel turned back to the patient, his brow tightening with tension as he called on all his intensive care skills to work to salvage the rapidly developing disaster in front of him.

Gaile Donovan had two young teenage daughters and a loving husband waiting anxiously in the waiting room for news of their loved one's condition. Gaile's cancer diagnosis had been bad enough, but to suffer this complication during surgery added an element of potential tragedy that would be very hard to announce to the family if things didn't go well.

With the help of Danielle and the nursing staff, he

replaced Allegra's previously inserted central line over a guide-wire and ensured it was running rapidly.

'Danielle, increase the noradrenaline infusion to three now, please, to help maintain blood pressure. I'm starting a vasopressin infusion to reduce venous pressure in the pelvis,' Joel instructed.

'Dr Addison, she's bleeding from every puncture site,' Danielle observed with growing alarm.

Despite massive transfusion, it was clear to Joel that coagulopathy was developing, and his inner tension went up another notch. Gaile's young daughters' faces swam before his eyes and his stomach clenched uncomfortably at the thought of having to face them with the worst news in the world.

'Unless we get this blood loss stopped now, no amount of intensive care is going to help her,' he said. Turning to the nurse at his side, he instructed, 'Get me four packs of FFP and I'll call the blood bank myself to retrieve ten packs of platelets.'

The ICTU nurse left to retrieve the packs of fresh-frozen plasma, which were stored in the ICTU blood fridge, as Joel reached for the nearest telephone.

A few minutes later a courier came in with the thawed platelets and Joel stabilised the patient to the point where she could be transferred to the operating theatre for a further attempt at pelvic packing and possible embolisation.

In Theatre, Allegra had set up the anesthetic machine, arterial line and monitoring equipment, and Harry and the scrub team were already scrubbed and waiting.

'She's extremely unstable, Dr Tallis—I'm just keeping up with fluids and she's coagulopathic. She's on norad at three and a vasopressin infusion. I've got FFP and platelets running and we're onto unit ten of fresh B blood, with ten left to go. Blood bank is scouring for more,' Joel said as the patient was transferred to the operating table.

Allegra gave him a worried look. 'I've really got my hands full here. Once we open up, her BP is going to hit the floor again.'

'I know that. I'll stay here and help with fluid and coag management while you manage the anesthesia,' he offered.

'That's a first,' Harry said, as the scrub nurse handed him scissors to open the previous incision. 'You don't often see an intensivist in Theatre.'

'That's the whole point of this new unit,' Joel said, as he assisted Allegra to attach the arterial line and monitor. 'Overlap of skills to break down the rigid barriers between specialties.'

While Allegra concentrated on anesthesia, Joel juggled fluid input, coagulation factors, consultation with the haematologists and blood bank, and provided general support to Allegra during the procedure. After rapid prepping and draping of the abdomen, Harry opened the previous incision to be greeted by welling up of venous blood from the pelvis.

'Her blood pressure's 60, Dr Addison,' Allegra said with concern, as she pumped in blood through two lines.

'Harry, we're not winning up this end. Can you control anything down there?' Joel asked over the drapes.

'I'm doing my best, guys, but there's no one bleeding point,' Harry rasped back, beads of sweat appearing on his brow above his mask.

Harry rapidly removed the old packs and repacked the pelvis, this time using multiple thumbtack-shaped staples to pin down every obvious bleeding vein to the pelvic walls before compressing with packs. In addition he ligated both internal iliac arteries. Although a drastic step, the bleeding finally slowed then stopped with repacking the pelvis.

'I can see clotting. You must have improved her

coag profile significantly,' Harry said with obvious relief in his eyes as they connected briefly with Joel and Allegra's.

'She's just about used up the entire supply of platelets and FFP. I think she'll run into ARDS after all of this,' Joel said.

'Her ventilation pressures are up, she's got pulmonary oedema—she's already in respiratory distress. I appreciate your help in Theatre, Dr Addison, but I'll be fine in here now. I'm sure you've got other concerns in the unit apart from this one patient,' Allegra said with brisk formality.

Joel gave her an indecipherable look before shifting his gaze towards the surgeon. 'See you later, Harry. Good luck with the rest of the procedure.'

'Yeah, thanks, Joel. I think I like this cross-over idea, ICU, anaesthesia and Theatre all in one for this sort of case. I just hope this poor lady makes it. She's put up one hell of a fight so far.'

'It's not over till it's over,' Joel said as he shed his theatre overgear and dropped it into the bins as he went. 'I'll speak to the relatives if you want me to, and then I'll do a quick change-over round with Tony Ringer before I leave.'

'No, don't worry, Joel, I'll see them. It's my responsibility,' Harry replied.

Joel nodded and left the theatre.

Harry looked at Allegra once Joel had left. 'I know I've said it before, but you two work well as a team,' he remarked. 'Are the rumours true, then?'

Allegra gave him a quelling look. 'I thought it was only the nursing staff who indulged in such a useless pastime as gossip.'

'In spite of your little formal act just then, anyone can see you and he have something going on.'

'Yes—an argument,' she said.

'He's a nice chap,' Harry said, as the nurse handed him another pack. 'I've worked under a lot of directors in the past but I can tell Joel Addison is switched on.'

'He's highly skilled, yes,' Allegra agreed, not quite able to disguise a little scowl.

Harry gave her another quick glance before he positioned another pack in the patient's abdomen. 'Are you still worried he's going to stop your project?'

'He's not keen on me working with the Lowe boy, especially now.'

'That's to be expected, I guess,' Harry said. 'God, it was a shock to think someone could waltz in and interfere with equipment like that on the mother. Have the police got any idea of who did it?'

'Not that I know of.'

'What about the father?' Harry asked. 'He's certainly got a motive, I would think.'

'He's also got an alibi,' Allegra pointed out.

Harry gave a grunt as he began to close the abdomen. 'How very convenient for him.'

'I don't think he did it,' she said, hoping her gut feeling was right.

'Not personally, but perhaps he had someone do it for him,' Harry said.

Allegra frowned as she checked the anaesthetic monitors. The same thought had crossed her own mind. Had Keith organised someone to get rid of his wife? It was clear he hated her for what she'd done to their son and if Tommy's injuries proved to be permanent, how much more would he want to avenge his son's life?

'What if he was the one who drugged her up and sent her off in that car in the first place?' Harry said into the silence.

Allegra swung back to look at him. 'With his own son sitting in the back seat? Come on, Harry. Keith might not win the husband-of-the-year award, but he loves his son. Besides, he wants me to do what I can to get Tommy to wake from his coma. If he was involved in any way with his wife's accident, I hardly think he'd want a seven-year-old witness on hand to testify against him.'

'Yeah, I guess you're right,' Harry said. 'But it pays to look at it from all angles.'

'That's what the police are for. There's already been too much gossip and innuendo as it is.'

'Speaking of gossip, Patrick Naylor was crowing about you and him having a drink later this evening,' he said as he finished closing the wound.

Allegra let out a frustrated breath as she began to reverse the anaesthetic. 'I'm only having a drink with him because he's been supportive of my project, although he's wavering on it in the Lowe boy case. It seems he's joined the Addison camp.'

Harry removed his mask and stripped off his gloves. 'There was a lot of opposition to your project, as you know. It was good of Patrick to stand by you, no matter what his motives.'

'What's your opinion, Harry?' she asked. 'Were you for or against my study?'

'Look, Allegra, you know I'm not one for reading auras or any of that stuff, but what you did with the Greeson girl was beyond what anyone else in the unit could offer. Her parents drew a lot of comfort from how you handled things. Even if your study goes on to prove nothing of scientific value, who's to say it's not worthwhile? Everyone wants results these days but sometimes we have to settle for what is. You helped two devastated parents cope with the worst tragedy imaginable, and you did it by maintaining their daughter's dignity right to the very end. So, yes, I was for your study, and still am.'

She gave him a grateful smile. 'Thanks, Harry.'

He winked at her. 'You remind me of my eldest daughter, Amelia. She wants to take on the world, and heaven help anyone who gets in her way.'

'The only person in my way is Joel Addison,' she said, with another downturn of her mouth.

'He's not in your way, Allegra,' Harry said. 'He's just trying to make sure the unit brings in the results everyone is expecting. I know you would have preferred Dougal Brenton but personally I think Joel Addison is streets ahead. He's had experience in a war-torn country and he's got a clear, calm head under pressure. He's innovative and focused, which is exactly what this hospital needs in its ICTU director right now.'

'I know all that but he has such a bias against me,' she said. 'I don't know how to get through to him.'

'I don't think you need to worry about getting his attention, Allegra,' he said with a grin. 'It seems obvious to me that you've certainly got that.'

She gave him a speaking glance. 'I've got his attention, but for all the wrong reasons.'

'I don't know about that. He's a reasonable enough man. If you can produce results, I think he'll come round.'

'I need more time to produce the sort of results he requires,' she said. 'It can take some patients weeks, if not months to regain consciousness. He's given me a month, but it's not long enough to do what I want to do.'

'Just do what you can in the time you have. You've got a chance with the Lowe kid—he's young and his brain damage may not be as bad as first expected. I've seen kids like him on ventilators for weeks and then suddenly they're up and running about as if nothing had happened.'

'I hope that's how it will be for Tommy,' she said. 'He's just seven years old.'

Harry gave her a probing look. 'You're not getting too emotionally involved in this, are you, Allegra? I know you had a rough time with the Greeson girl but we all have to move on. They're our patients and we do what we can, but it's not our fault if we can't pull a miracle out of the hat every time.'

'No, I'm fine,' she said, wondering if it was true.

'I just want to give this my best shot. I know there's potential in this study. I can sense it.'

'You have to show it, not sense it,' he reminded her, with scientific pragmatism.

'I know that, Harry. I'm well aware of the parameters I have to work within. I just think there are ways we're not utilising that could help patients regain consciousness. Everything seems to be economically rationalised these days—if there's no EEG activity after X days and Y dollars of ICU support, pull the plug. But with a different theoretical approach and some time and effort, I believe we could start a paradigm shift in the management of post-traumatic coma.'

'I hope to God you're right, Allegra,' he said, as he removed his surgical gown. 'I hate it when ventilators are switched off on live bodies. It doesn't matter how many CT scans and EEGs, I still can't help feeling there might have been…' He didn't need to complete the sentence.

'I know,' she said with a heartfelt sigh. '"Brain dead" is a cold, hard term. I realise we can't keep people alive indefinitely on a ventilator when there's clearly no hope. I just want to make absolutely sure there *is* no hope, that we're covering every aspect, not giving up before every option is explored.'

'I know it's a well-worn adage, but I really do believe that where there's life there's hope. Joel was right when he said earlier that it's not over until it's over. Even Gaile Donovan here—sick as she is—still has a slim chance of making it.'

Allegra looked down at the pallid features of the patient under her care. 'I certainly hope so, Harry.'

He gave her a weary glance as he helped move the patient from the operating table to the ICTU bed. 'I'm going out to speak to the husband and daughters now. I wish I could promise them more but I'm not a miracle-worker.'

'She's alive, Harry,' Allegra said. 'That's all that matters right now. That's all they'll want to hear.'

'I know, but for how long?' he asked as she wheeled the patient past him out of Theatre.

Allegra didn't answer. She didn't like Gaile Donovan's chances either, but to voice them seemed to be inviting the worst. She'd already had enough of the worst. What she needed now was a miracle and she was going to go looking for it, no matter what Joel Addison said to the contrary.

CHAPTER TEN

PATRICK Naylor was sitting in the bar, waiting for her, when Allegra finally arrived, the two empty glasses in front of him suggesting he'd been there for quite a while.

'I'm sorry I'm late but I had to go back to Theatre,' she said as she sat down opposite him.

'I wasn't worried…not really,' he said, giving her a quick on-off smile before his eyes moved away from hers as he stared into the empty glass in front of him, his shoulders suddenly slumping. 'I just needed to see a friendly face.'

'Is everything all right, Patrick?' Allegra asked.

He gradually brought his gaze back to hers, the moisture shining there indicating he was having trouble keeping his emotions at bay. 'My wife is pregnant to her lover,' he said. 'I found out about it this morning.'

'I'm so sorry. That must be awful for you.'

He wiped at his eyes with the back of his hand. 'The irony is it was me who kept putting off having a family. I guess that's why she went looking elsewhere.'

She reached for his hand and gave it a gentle squeeze. 'Is there anything I can do?'

He shook his head and covered her hand with his. 'No, there's nothing anyone can do. I have to deal with it myself.' He released a little sigh and continued, 'I've booked in to see a counsellor. I think it's time I did some work on myself.'

'That's very brave of you,' she said softly.

He removed his hand from hers. 'I'm sorry I've been so full on lately. I thought if I threw myself into a new relationship I wouldn't feel so bad about it all.'

'I understand.'

He gave her a twisted, somewhat grim smile. 'I wanted to make my wife jealous. I thought if she saw you hanging on my arm she'd change her mind and come back, but that's not going to happen now. It's over.'

'I'm glad you explained it to me.'

'There's something else...' He pushed his empty glass out of his reach before his eyes returned to hers. 'Joel Addison didn't ask you out for the reasons I said. He is concerned about some issues pertaining to your project, especially since the Lowe incident, but I was just jealous and wanted to cause trouble.'

'Oh…'

'It was pathetic, I know, and I'm ashamed of myself. I hope I haven't made things difficult for you. I know you have to work pretty closely with him.'

'I'm sure we'll sort it out…' Allegra said, already mentally rehearsing an apology as she recalled her heated interaction with Joel earlier.

Patrick got to his feet and, leaning down, placed a quick peck on her cheek before straightening. 'Thanks for listening, Allegra. See you around some time.'

'Be kind to yourself, Patrick. These things take time. Bye.'

Joel wrote up the last of his notes before leaning back in his chair with a tired sigh. He rubbed his face, grimacing at the sound of his palm on his unshaven jaw. His conversation with Anthony Pardle about Tommy Lowe hadn't been encouraging. There didn't seem to be much hope but Joel had wanted to make sure he wasn't allowing his personal feelings get in the way. He had rearranged the shifts so the more experienced nurses were looking after the little boy and he had restricted visitors so that noise and disruption was at a minimum.

He'd even spent some time with the little boy after Anthony had left, sitting by his bed, talking to him, telling him some of the stuff he used to do as a kid.

'I had a bike, a red one with blue stripes,' he'd said, holding the boy's small hand in his. 'I thought I was pretty cool, riding up and down the street while my brother watched on the sidelines.'

A nurse had come past and he waited until she'd moved on before continuing in a low, urgent tone, 'Come on, Tommy, you have to do your best, mate, to wake up. No half-measures, got that?' He gave the little hand in his a gentle squeeze. 'I'm counting on you to pull out of this. You have to do it, for yourself, not just for your parents and Dr Tallis. You have to do it for yourself.'

'How's Tommy doing?' Allegra asked Bethany, when she returned to ICTU before heading home for the night.

The nurse handed her the BIS readouts. 'No sign of any brain activity, I'm afraid.'

Allegra fought against her disappointment as she read the printout.

'The movie finished a while ago,' Bethany said. 'Do you want me to rerun it?'

'Yes—it can't hurt to give it another go,' she said, still hoping for a miracle.

'Anthony Pardle came in a little while ago,' Bethany informed her. 'I overheard him talking to Dr Addison about Tommy.'

'What did he say?'

'He doesn't think there's much hope of Tommy recovering.'

Allegra refused to be put off. 'You know what neurosurgeons are like—they see the worst so they always imagine the worst.'

'Maybe, but Dr Addison seemed to be in agreement with him,' Bethany said. 'He agreed with Mr Pardle that Mr Lowe should be informed of the possibility of withdrawing life support from his son.'

Allegra felt her stomach drop in alarm. *'So soon?'*

'Brain dead is brain dead, Allegra,' Bethany said. 'An hour, a day, a week or a month won't make Tommy's brain repair itself.'

'But it's only been a couple of days!' she argued. 'We normally give patients a week or ten days before making that sort of decision. Besides, he's a child. Studies have shown that children sometimes do recover from severe head trauma after prolonged support.'

'I know, but Dr Addison and Mr Pardle have the final say, in consultation with the father, when they think the time is right,' Bethany reminded her. 'The sad thing is the mother is starting to show signs of regaining consciousness. It doesn't seem fair that she gets another chance at life when her son doesn't.'

'What's been happening with Kate Lowe?'

'They've withdrawn the barbiturates, as we have with Tommy, but while in Tommy's case nothing has happened, Kate has shown signs of spontaneous breathing and she opened her eyes once.'

'And her BIS monitor scores?'

'There are definite signs of brain activity,' Bethany said. 'But not in Tommy's.'

Allegra compressed her lips together as she looked at the small child being kept alive, his tiny limbs seeming to be even smaller than the day before. 'Come on, Tommy,' she pleaded softly. 'Wake up, honey. I know you can do it.'

Bethany gave Allegra a surreptitious nudge. 'Here comes Tommy's father and his aunt.'

'Dr Tallis,' Keith greeted her. 'I'd like you to meet my sister, Serena Fairbright.'

'Hello,' Allegra said, offering her hand to the glamorous woman accompanying Tommy's father.

Serena's hand brushed Allegra's briefly. 'How is my little nephew?'

'He's doing as well as can be expected,' Allegra answered.

'How did you go with the movie?' Keith asked.

'We're playing it again now.'

'So he hasn't responded?' Keith asked.

'No, but I'd like your permission to try a couple of other things,' Allegra said. 'Firstly I would like to try a particular massage therapy to see if he responds.'

'Massage?' Serena gave a sceptical frown. 'How is that going to repair his head injury?'

'Children are very touch-sensitive,' Allegra explained. 'Young children in particular are used to being touched by their mother and father in loving ways, such as helping them dress each morning, doing their hair for them or cuddling them.'

'Look, Dr Tallis, I'm not a new-age sort of man, as you've probably already guessed,' Keith confessed. 'I was brought up by strict parents who only ever touched me with a strap or a belt in their hands. I find it hard to express physical affection. I've never really kissed or cuddled Tommy, or at least not since he was about a year old.'

'I know this is painful for you to answer, but did his mother have any particular physical routine that you can recall that Tommy might respond to?' Allegra asked.

He gave her a shamefaced look. 'I was always on at Kate for being too soft on the boy,' he said. 'She was always touching him, kissing him or playing with his hair. I was frightened she would make a sissy out of him.'

'A lot of men feel that way, but let me assure you nothing could be further from the truth,' Allegra said. 'Touch is essential in a child's life. Why not sit with Tommy now and tell him you're here? And if you feel up to it, touch him in any way that makes you feel comfortable.'

'We haven't got long,' Serena said, with an impatient glance at her diamond-encrusted watch.

'If you think it would help…' Keith said, although he looked as doubtful as his sister.

Allegra left them in privacy to return to the office, where she made a few notes, but she'd hardly finished a sentence or two when she saw Keith and his sister leave the unit once more.

'What did I tell you?' Bethany said poking her head around the glass partition. 'She's exactly the same as him—cold as a frozen fish.'

'Yes, well, with that sort of background, what else could you expect?' Allegra said as she toyed with her pen. 'I can't believe how cruel some parents can be. It's no wonder Mr Lowe didn't want Tommy's grandparents to be contacted.'

'I guess you're right,' Bethany said. 'Well, I'm off now that Chloe's back. I did an extra couple of hours to cover for her. Dr Addison is insisting only the senior staff look after Tommy.'

Allegra looked up at that. 'Oh?'

'Yes, he may not be too keen on your project, but he's certainly doing his best to help Tommy before he makes his final decision. I saw him sitting with him earlier. He was talking to him and stroking his hand. If you ask me, he was a whole lot better at it than the kid's own father.'

'Thanks for helping with Tommy,' Allegra said after a tiny pause. 'I'm going to head off home.'

'No hot date tonight?'

'I have a date with a good book and a glass of Pinot noir,' she answered. 'That's about as hot as it gets in my life right now.'

'You could always throw a vindaloo curry in there somewhere to turn up the heat a bit,' Bethany suggested with a smile.

'What a great idea,' Allegra said, as she dragged

herself to her feet. 'The last thing I want to do is cook. Take-away, here I come.'

The Indian restaurant not far from her apartment had a small waiting area for customers waiting for their take-out orders. Allegra sank gratefully into a vinyl chair once she'd placed her order and picked up a magazine that was at least two years out of date, flicking through it absently.

Once her number was called she collected her meal and made her way out to the street, but had only gone a few paces when she saw a very familiar figure heading her way.

Joel looked down at the container in her hand. 'Great minds think alike, it seems,' he said. 'What did you get?'

'Beef vindaloo.'

'Enough for two?'

'No.'

'Pity,' he said. 'I guess I'll have to go and order my own.'

She pursed her lips for a moment. 'I suppose I could make it stretch, but only if you've got a decent bottle of wine.'

He gave her a smile that melted her instantly. 'I'll go and get one from the bottle shop and meet you back at your place. Is there anything else you need?'

Only my head read, she thought as she returned his smile with a tentative one of her own. 'No, the wine will be fine.'

Allegra answered the door a short time later and he held out the bottle for her to inspect. 'Mmm…' She peered at the label. 'Last Hope Ridge, a '98 Merlot. Not a bad vintage. You have good taste.'

'In some things,' he said, looking down at the soft curve of her mouth.

Allegra felt her senses spring to attention at the smouldering heat in his dark gaze as it returned to hers, her skin feeling tight and overly sensitive, as if preparing itself for his touch.

'So I take it internet dating didn't work out?' she said, surprised her voice sounded so normal when her breathing was all over the place.

'I was seriously thinking about it,' he said, stepping closer. 'But I wasn't sure if you'd cast a spell on me earlier today so that I would end up with some wacko woman intent on having her wicked way with me.'

'I do not cast spells,' she said, trying to sound cross and indignant, but it didn't quite work, with him smiling at her so disarmingly.

'Yes, you do,' he said, tugging her closer, his hands on her hips. 'You're doing it right now.'

'That's totally ridiculous,' she gasped as his lower body came into contact with hers. 'I wouldn't know the first thing about magic…and all that…stuff…' She swallowed as he brought his head down, his warm breath caressing the surface of her lips.

'What about this stuff?' he asked, as his mouth brushed hers.

'That's not magic…' she breathed into his mouth.

'What is it, then?' he asked, his warm breath mingling with hers.

'It's…madness…' she said, kissing him back softly, her lips clinging to his. 'Total madness…'

'It's not madness,' he growled as he pulled her even closer. 'It's desire.'

'Lust,' she corrected him. 'It's good old-fashioned lust. It will go away if we ignore it.'

'How do you suggest we ignore it?' he asked, nibbling gently at the soft underside of her neck.

'Um…we could try some other activity…' She shivered all over as the tip of his tongue briefly entered her ear.

'What did you have in mind?' He grazed her top lip with the masculine and totally irresistible rasp of his tongue. 'Scrabble?'

'I cheat at Scrabble,' she said, sagging against him as he found her bottom lip and stroked it with his tongue, back and forth until her lip began to swell with need. 'I make up words and I always win.'

'I'd never let you get away with it,' he warned softly, as his mouth hovered over hers.

'No one's beaten me yet.' Her breath mingled intimately with his, making her stomach feel hollow.

'I like the sound of being the first to conquer you,' he said, pressing his mouth to hers in a scorching, probing kiss that left her totally breathless. Her arms wound around his neck as she rose on tiptoe to get even closer to him, her fingers delving into the thick black pelt of his hair, her body soft against his hardness, her legs feeling unsteady and trembling with desire.

He lifted his mouth from hers after endless minutes, his dark eyes alight with rampant need as they locked on hers. 'We should eat before this gets out of hand. We've both had a long day and we're not thinking with our heads here.'

'You're right,' she said, unwinding her arms from his neck and stepping back from him. 'Besides, I need to get an apology out of the way.'

'What do you need to apologise for?'

'Patrick told me you had only asked me out to

keep me away from the unit. I was angry with you for exploiting me without checking to see if what he'd said was actually right.'

'I see.'

'He apologised for it earlier this evening. He's going through a rough time in his personal life.'

'And here I was thinking it was my kisses that finally convinced you of my motives,' he said, with a wry twist to his mouth.

'Your kisses are definitely very convincing,' she admitted, lowering her eyes from the steadiness of his. 'But…but aren't we rushing things a bit?'

'What do you mean?'

She raised her eyes back to encounter his unwavering dark brown gaze. 'We may be attracted to each other physically, but we're poles apart professionally. You have issues with my study and I have issues over your decision to withdraw life support on Tommy Lowe. This is never going to work between us.'

'Come on, Allegra.' His tone became impatient. 'You know the routine with head injuries. Once the patient is declared brain dead by the neurosurgeon we have no choice but to advise the relatives to consider withdrawing life support. It's not fair to the patient or the relatives to let them hang in limbo for no gain.'

'Tommy is a young child,' she countered. 'Numerous studies have demonstrated the possibility of recovery after more prolonged support in children.'

'Yes, but exactly what sort of recovery are we talking about?'

'A full recovery, of course.'

He let out a short rough expletive. 'You really are off with the fairies, aren't you? Damn it, Allegra, you know there are degrees of recovery in these sorts of cases. Tommy could end up permanently disabled, either physically or intellectually or, God help him, both. He'd be totally dependent on his father or his mother if she survives. What sort of life is that for any of them?'

'He'd be alive, that's all that matters to a parent,' she argued.

'Is it?' he asked, his eyes glittering with some indefinable pent-up emotion she couldn't quite recognise.

'Of course it is! Losing a child is the most devastating thing that can happen to a parent. The grief is total and all-consuming.'

'So is the grief of being totally responsible for a child who will never grow up, either physically or mentally,' he said, grasping her by the upper arms, his fingers biting into her tender flesh. 'Have you thought about that any time in your fairy-dust study? Have you ever interviewed the relatives of a child who didn't get your magical full recovery? Have you asked them what it's like to have to change their adult child's nappy several times a day, to spoon food and drink into them while most of it dribbles down their chin? Have you asked them what it's like to lie awake at night, listening to their child uttering screams and cries that no physical comfort or words will ever ease? Have you asked them what it's like for the rest of the family, their marriage, and all their other relation-ships? *Have you?*'

She shrank back from the vitriol in his tone. 'I— I… No I haven't, but I—'

He dropped his hands from her so suddenly she almost stumbled backwards. 'You don't know what you're doing, Allegra. I could see that from the first moment I looked at your study. You can't keep people alive indefinitely without weighing the costs.'

'Neither can you play God,' she said. 'You can't possibly think it's reasonable to wander through ICU and switch off ventilators, without giving the relatives adequate time to make that decision if it's called for.'

'Tommy Lowe will be given the same time frame every other patient in his condition is given. But once ten days is up, if there is still no brain activity his father will be informed of his choices. We can keep that child alive for months, but while he's soaking up valuable resources, three or four other children will die for want of organ donation that Tommy's brain-dead body could provide. Why don't you go and visit some of them in the children's ward? Have a talk to the parents sitting there hour after hour, with the clock on the wall ticking away their child's last chance at a normal life.'

Allegra knew his argument was reasonable; she was well aware of the lifesaving transplants that offered hope when all else had failed. It was, after all, sometimes the only comfort in losing a loved one to know that some part of them lived on, giving precious life to some other person who then could go on to live a normal life. Julie's parents had made the very same difficult decision when their daughter's ventilator had finally been switched off. But Allegra had always thought Julie had deserved more time. It gnawed at her constantly. She couldn't help feeling her friend's parents had been pressured into their final decision.

'I understand what you're saying, but I still think

your bias against me is colouring your judgement,' she said. 'All I'm asking is for some extra time to work with Tommy.'

'You've got a week,' he said, moving past her to the door. 'Ten days at the most, and then Anthony Pardle and I will have to organise a meeting with the father.'

She swung around to look at him. 'You don't have to leave—I thought we were having dinner?'

He gave her one hard look and opened the door. 'Maybe some other time. I seem to have lost my appetite.'

She frowned as he closed the door, the sound of his footsteps gradually fading before she turned and leaned back against the door, her shoulders slumping despondently against the hard surface. 'Help me to prove him wrong, Tommy,' she said out loud, the words bouncing eerily off the stony silence of the walls.

CHAPTER ELEVEN

ALLEGRA arrived in ICTU the following morning well before her shift officially began, and painstakingly looked through the printouts on Tommy's BIS monitor. There had been no change, which was dispiriting enough, but with the deadline Joel had now attached to the case, the sense of urgency seemed all the more gut-wrenching. She had hardly slept for thinking about the little boy's life, how he would look in five, ten years' time if he survived. Would he retain the slight build of his mother, or during adolescence develop the shorter and thicker set of his father? Would he do well at school? What sort of sense of humour would he have?

And what about his aunt? Was Tommy close to her? Did he understand at his young age the difficulties of his father's relationship with his own parents, Tommy's grandparents? Did he see much of his mother's parents and if not, why not?

There were so many unanswerable questions that she was finding difficult enough—how much worse would it be being the parent and never having those questions answered? She had seen that level of devastating grief on the faces of Julie's parents all those years ago and more recently on the faces of Robyn and Jeff Greeson as their precious daughter's chest had moved up and down for the very last time. Allegra had seen the pain flash across their faces as they'd come to terms with the fact that they would never know what their daughter would have looked like on her wedding day, never know what sort of man she would have fallen in love with. Every birthday, Christmas or special anniversary would no longer be a cause for celebration but a reminder of their unrelenting pain.

Statistics showed most couples didn't survive the loss of a child and it was easy to see why. The burden of grief was like a sharp, invisible knife that progressively severed the ties of even the closest couple with cruelly isolating dissection. Allegra had felt it herself all the way through medical school and beyond. She'd felt as if she'd been walled inside a see-through barrier that no one could penetrate. She'd been cut away from the rest of her peers by the experience of her closest friend's suicide, and her guilt and sense of inadequacy had been intensified by that ongoing isolation.

Allegra looked up from Tommy's notes to see Judy, the nurse in charge of Kate Lowe's room, approach. Judy had been the one who had been on duty when Kate Lowe's ventilator had been sabotaged two nights previously.

'Dr Tallis? You're in early this morning. I was just going to call you at home,' Judy said. 'I thought you might be interested in Mrs Lowe's current condition.'

'How is she?' Allegra asked.

'She's extubated, and drifting in and out of lucidity,' Judy informed her.

'Has she said anything at any time during her conscious times?'

'She's said Tommy's name several times and the nurse who covered for me over my break said she asked for Tommy's aunt once or twice. She hasn't said anything for several hours now but I thought you might be interested.'

'I am—very. How are you coping with all this?' she asked. 'Is this your first time taking care of a patient with a police guard present?'

'Here, it is, but at the previous hospital I worked at in Sydney I had to nurse a prisoner who had been injured in a cell brawl. But after what happened the other night, I'm glad someone is keeping watch. I still can't believe we almost lost her.'

Allegra leaned back in her chair and looked at the nurse intently. 'So you don't think she deserves to die for what she tried to do to her son?'

The nurse looked shocked. 'Of course not! I'm a mother myself. I've had some rough times, I can tell you, especially after my husband left me when my daughter was only three weeks old. I know what it's like to feel overwhelmed and depressed. There were numerous times when I seriously considered ending it all. I think if more women were honest about it, you'd find most would confess to having experienced the same feelings at times. I was lucky, I had a mother who saw the desperate state I was in and stepped in and took over until I got myself back on my feet. Others, like Kate Lowe, obviously don't have that supportive network. I feel sorry for her. No one has even called to ask after her, which shows how lonely and isolated she must have been at the time.'

'Yes, that does seem a little unusual,' Allegra put in. 'Even the most hardened criminals have relatives who love them and call and ask to see them.'

'Yes, that's true…' Judy gave her a pensive look. 'But the funny thing was during that time when I wanted to end it all I had systematically cut myself off from all of my friends. It's the irony of depression, I suppose. The one time in your life you need the loving support of people around to help, you actively push them away. I know I did it, often cruelly at times. A couple of my friends never quite forgave me for it. Maybe Kate over time has pushed everyone away, including her parents. Family feuds are all too common these days. Some people never speak to each other again. It's such a terrible shame.'

'I guess you're right…' Allegra said, as she got to her feet. She touched the nurse briefly on the arm and added sincerely, 'The world needs more people like you, Judy.'

Judy gave her a shy smile. 'I was just thinking that about you, Dr Tallis. I've been meaning to tell you how much I admired you for fighting for the opportunity to do this study. If I had taken the drastic step Kate Lowe did—and let me tell you I was close to it—I would have wanted someone like you to give me another chance.'

'We all deserve a second chance, Judy,' Allegra said. 'But unfortunately there's someone out there or even here in the hospital who doesn't think the same as you and I. They wanted Kate Lowe to die and if it hadn't been for you, she very well could have done so.'

'I hope the police find out who did it soon,' Judy said. 'It doesn't look good for the unit or the new director, does it?'

'No.' Allegra let out a little sigh as she thought of the immense pressure Joel was under. She had been too quick to judge him without considering how difficult things had been for him, newly appointed and with so many people's expectations burdening him. Every time she saw him he looked even more exhausted. No wonder he had been so short with her the night before. He wanted results and he wanted them quickly. And yet, in spite of his misgivings, he had ensured Tommy received only the best attention and care.

'I'm off home now,' Judy said, interrupting her reverie.

'Lucky you,' Allegra said, wincing as she looked up at the clock on the wall. 'I've only got thirteen and a half hours to go.'

The police officer guarding Kate Lowe's room looked up as Allegra came in after the mandatory security check. Allegra introduced herself and explained briefly about her study before she came over to the patient's bed and looked down at the young woman lying there. Without the hiss and groan of the ventilator, the room seemed extraordinarily quiet. The monitoring equipment still attached to Kate made her seem small and vulnerable, not unlike her little son further along the unit.

'Kate, my name is Allegra Tallis,' Allegra said, as she took one of the woman's hands in hers and stroked it gently. 'I'm a doctor, an anaesthetist, and I've been looking after your son, Tommy.'

Kate's eyelids fluttered for a moment, as if the mention of her son's name had stirred her from her unconscious state. Allegra waited for several moments before continuing in a soft, soothing voice, 'He's doing OK. I've been playing his favourite movie for him.'

Kate's mouth moved and a breathless, almost inaudible sound came out. 'Tommy…'

'Tommy is doing as well as can be expected, Kate,' Allegra reassured her, hoping that by saying the words it would someone make it true.

'Serena…' Kate's lips moved again but then she groaned and slipped back into unconsciousness.

Allegra stroked the woman's thin hands, using the massage technique she had been taught, separating each finger, stretching them gently, lengthening the tendons to release built-up pressure. She turned over Kate's hand palm upwards and froze when she saw a series of tiny, nick-like, whitened scars on the underside of the wrist. She reached for Kate's other arm and found the same bizarre pattern carved on the other wrist.

'She's a fruit cake,' Ruth Tilley, the nurse assigned to the isolation room, muttered under her breath, but even so it was more than obvious that the police officer had heard every word.

Allegra frowned as she turned to face the nurse. 'Please, keep your personal opinions to yourself. If you feel uncomfortable nursing this patient, I suggest you ask to be transferred.'

The nurse gave an insolent sniff and moved to check the monitors, making a note of Kate's BP, pulse and sats. 'I know how to do my job, no matter how horrible the patient is. Anyway, I've nursed much worse than her.'

'I would prefer you to speak appropriately and professionally at all times in this room,' Allegra insisted. 'Kate Lowe is unconscious but may well be able to hear everything you say.'

'I don't care if she does,' Ruth said. 'She's tried to do herself in numerous times. If she recovers, she'll only do it again. I've seen it all before. These sorts of people are nothing but trouble for their families. They put them through hell, keeping everyone on tenterhooks, wondering when the next attempt is going to happen and whether it will be successful.'

Allegra tightened her mouth as she saw the look the police officer gave the nurse, as if he was in silent agreement.

'Excuse me,' she said as she brushed past to leave. 'I have other patients to see.'

Once outside Kate's room Allegra expelled a frustrated breath, her hands clenching at her sides to keep control. She walked towards the office of ICTU where Louise was sitting, looking over the night shift notes.

'Uh-oh,' Louise said as she looked up. 'I don't like the look of your aura right now. I can practically see sparks of anger zapping off the top of your head. Has the dishy director got under your skin again?'

'Surprising as it may seem, no. It's not Joel this time—it's one of the nurses.'

'So we're on first-name terms, are we?' Louise asked with a playful smile.

Allegra ignored her friend's teasing look. 'I want Ruth Tilley removed from Kate Lowe's room immediately.'

Louise frowned. 'But why? Ruth is one of the most experienced ICTU nurses we have here.'

'I don't care how experienced she is, I don't like her attitude,' Allegra said. 'Has Joel Addison arrived yet?'

Louise's frown deepened. 'You're going to ask him to move her?'

'No,' she said, as she straightened her spine. 'I'm not going to ask him—I'm going to *tell* him.'

'I think he's headed down to Gaile Donovan's room. He's waiting for Harry Upton,' Louise said. 'The husband's been there all night. Joel came in early to discuss her treatment options with Harry.'

Joel looked up from Gaile Donovan's notes as Allegra entered the small private room where the patient was being closely monitored. 'Have you seen Harry come in yet?' he asked, without so much as offering a simple greeting.

'Good morning to you, too, Dr Addison,' Allegra said with an arch look.

He frowned and resumed looking at the notes. 'Sorry,' he said a little gruffly. 'I hadn't noticed it was even morning. I came in before the sun was up.'

Allegra felt annoyed with herself for being so petty when it was clear Joel had bigger concerns on his mind, such as the patient lying between them. But before she could offer an apology, Harry Upton came in.

'Morning, Allegra, Joel. How were things overnight with Gaile Donovan?'

'She's been stable, Harry,' Joel answered. 'Certainly no more bleeding, but Allegra was right about the ARDS. We did a chest X-ray this morning and there is a virtual white-out of most of both lung fields.'

Allegra checked the ventilator readings and reported, 'Her ventilation pressures are high and she's needing 40 per cent oxygen.'

'What about coagulopathy?' Harry asked. 'At some stage in the next 48 hours I'm going to have to remove the pelvic packs. How are we placed timing-wise?'

'She's stable at the moment and we've got her on broad-spectrum antibiotic cover,' Joel said. 'My advice would be to leave things alone the full 48 hours. Coags are better than they were, but PT is still prolonged and her platelets are low. We can work at improving those and hope her chest improves, before subjecting her to the potential of another hypovolaemic insult.' He turned his gaze towards Allegra. 'Do you agree, Allegra?'

'Yes.' Allegra was momentarily taken aback by the dark shadows beneath his eyes. He looked like she felt—tired, defeated, and a little out of his depth. It made him seem less of an enemy and she felt something that had been previously hard and closed off inside her begin to soften a little. She suddenly became aware of both Harry's and Joel's expectant gazes trained on her. 'Um…yes, I would prefer not to have to reanaesthetise her until we see how the lung function pans out.'

Joel shifted his gaze and checked the obs with the attending nurse, Jayne Stephens. He listened to Gaile's chest but there was very little in terms of air entry, and a lot of crackles and crepitations. He knew Gaile was in for a rough ride but he had seen such patients recover with adequate ICU support— the key was to avoid sepsis and maintain organ support and brain oxygenation.

'We should go and have a chat with her husband,' he suggested, once he'd finished his checks. 'He's been here all night. I sent him out to the conference room a few minutes ago to stretch his legs.'

Harry's beeper went off and he grimaced as he looked at the screen. 'Sorry, guys, I've got a surgical tutorial with the trainees and I'm already ten minutes late. You know what these young folk are like—if we don't turn up on the dot they think we've cancelled and go off and have a latte instead.'

Joel smiled at the older surgeon. 'Can't say I blame them. I could do with a double-strength latte myself right now.' He turned to Allegra once Harry had left, his easy smile replaced by a little frown. 'Do you want to come with me to talk to Neil Donovan or is a coffee more preferable?'

'I was coming to see you anyway about another matter,' she said. 'After we've spoken with Mr Donovan, perhaps you could fit me into your busy schedule.'

He gave her an unreadable look as he held the door for her. 'I'll see what I can do.'

They moved from the unit past the security guard to the conference room along the corridor, where Neil Donovan was sitting with his head in his hands. He looked up as they came in, the dread on his face clawing at Allegra's already overstretched emotions.

'How are you holding up?' Joel asked.

'I'm just hoping she's going to be OK,' Neil said, his eyes red and weary beyond description. 'The girls and I just couldn't go on if…' His voice trailed off and Allegra swallowed against the lump in her throat.

'She's been stable overnight, Neil,' Joel informed him, closing the small distance to place a reassuring hand on his shoulder. 'That's positive. She's getting the best talent this hospital has.'

'I know...' Neil said, not bothering to disguise the track of tears moving down his unshaven cheeks. 'I just hope it's enough. I'm not a religious man but I've been praying all night for a miracle.'

Joel glanced briefly in Allegra's direction. 'Miracles are hard to arrange, Neil. Maybe they happen—certainly some people believe in them. Try to hold onto hope. There's still a decent chance she can pull through. We'll explore every feasible option.'

'Can I go back to her now?' Neil asked.

'Of course you can.' Joel smiled warmly. 'Who's looking after the girls for you?'

'I left them with my mother, although they weren't too happy about it,' Neil said.

'If they want to be here with their mother, that's where they should be,' Joel said. 'If there's anything you want any of us to do, just let us know.'

'Thank you, Dr Addison. You, too, Dr Tallis,' he said. 'I don't know how you doctors deal with this stuff day in and day out. It must really get to you after a while.'

'We're trained to cope with it,' Joel said. 'Mind you, it's totally different when you're on the other side. I haven't as yet been a patient myself, but I've had plenty of practice at being a patient's relative. It's a tough call. You're doing a great job, Neil. Your ongoing support is just what your wife needs right now.'

Neil Donovan gave them both a tired smile and, thanking them again, left to be with his wife back in the unit.

'He's certainly a very different kettle of fish to our friend Mr Lowe,' Allegra couldn't help commenting as the door closed on his exit.

Joel turned and looked down at her, his nostrils instinctively flaring so he could take in more of her light perfume. It reminded him of freshly cut spring flowers warmed by the sun, heady and evocative without being too overpowering. He wanted to haul her into his arms and kiss her deeply so he could carry the sweet tantalising taste of her throughout the long, arduous day ahead. His groin tightened at the thought of slipping his tongue inside her mouth to curl around hers, the palms of his hands sliding under her clothes to cover her breasts to feel their softness crowned with her hardened nipples.

With a gargantuan effort he forced the images of their bodies locked in passion from his mind and asked, 'What did you want to see me about?'

'I want you to remove Ruth Tilley from Kate

Lowe's room,' she said implacably. 'In fact, not just Kate's room but ICTU altogether.'

His brow wrinkled as he brought the senior nurse's features to mind, mentally reminding himself of her impressive capabilities. He'd seen her manage a trauma patient with multiple injuries almost single-handedly the previous week when several multi-trauma patients had arrived simultaneously and the medical staff had been stretched beyond the limits. She had saved a young man's life and surely didn't deserve the indignity of being dismissed from the unit without a very good reason.

'Why? Have you some sort of issue with her?'

'Yes, I do, actually. She's got the wrong attitude.'

His features hardened. 'According to who?'

Allegra could feel his intransigence like an impenetrable wall being built brick by brick between them. She drew herself up to her full height and bit out, 'According to me.'

'Let me guess.' His mouth quirked a fraction. 'Her aura is off centre, is it?'

Allegra had had enough. 'Don't you dare make fun of me, Addison. If anyone's aura is askew, it's yours.'

He looked down at her flashing green eyes and his smile tilted even further. 'Are you threatening me, Dr Tallis?'

She held his taunting brown gaze for several heart-chugging seconds, the atmosphere tightening around them to snapping point. The air was thick with it. She couldn't even breathe properly. Her chest felt restricted, her head light as if not enough oxygen was getting through to her brain. Deep and low in her belly a throbbing pulse had begun a tattoo that triggered a silky liquid response between her thighs, which she suddenly realised with a jolt of awareness were way too close to his. Their hard muscled presence alerted her too late to the hot sexual current charging between their bodies, a current that she had tried desperately to ignore because of what she knew it signified.

She tried to step back but both of his hands countered it by coming down on her hips and with one short hard tug bringing her up against him.

'Who's going to throw the first punch, Allegra?' he asked, staring at her mouth as if mesmerised. 'Or should we kiss and make up instead?'

She moistened her lips nervously, her heart leaping in her chest as he brought his head down, her breath consumed by the greedy hunger of his mouth as it captured hers.

CHAPTER TWELVE

His kiss was a searing reminder of her escalating feelings for him, feelings she had never expected to feel for anyone, or at least not at this level of intensity. She wasn't cynical enough to discount the prospect of ever falling in love, but never had she expected to do so in such a short space of time. She had not been in love with anyone before, although she had slept with previous boyfriends, more because of their expectations than anything she'd felt herself. But somehow Joel Addison, the one man who stood in the way of what she wanted to achieve, had stolen her heart without her being able to do anything to prevent it. She hadn't even seen it coming. It had crept up on her with every look he'd sent her way, every word he'd spoken and with every nuance of his face as she'd watched him deal sensitively with patients and relatives and staff.

She wasn't fool enough to imagine he had similar

feelings for her. She knew enough about male hormones to recognise full-on lust when she saw it. Every determined stroke of his tongue against hers reminded her of how his body would feel inside the silky cocoon of hers. No rational argument was going to be enough to fight this overwhelming attraction that had crackled constantly between them almost from the first moment they'd met.

She returned his kiss with the same fire as his, her tongue dancing with his, her small teeth nipping at his bottom lip in response to the similar tantalising treatment by his. It was a primitive sort of exchange, at times bordering on the edge of pain, as if they were both trying to find each other's boundaries.

Allegra imagined he would be a demanding but totally enthralling lover. She could feel it in his hands as they ruthlessly tugged her shirt out of her skirt, his warm palms possessing the aching weight of her breasts until her stomach caved in with out-of-control desire.

Her fingers curled into the thickness of his hair as she struggled to control her reaction to him. She was within a second of begging him to take her then and there when he dragged himself away to look down at her with glittering eyes, a dull flush of colour beneath the tan of his face.

'Maybe I should have let you punch me instead,' he said with a rueful smile that melted her almost as much as his kisses had done. 'It might have been less complicated.'

She tidied her clothes as best as she could, trying her best to sound casual even while her stomach was still crawling with desire. 'I don't believe in violence,' she said. 'I would never have hit you.'

'That's very reassuring. For a moment there I thought I was going to have to make an emergency appointment with my orthodontist.'

She gave him a shame-faced look from beneath her lashes as she tucked in her blouse with unsteady hands. 'I'm sorry. I didn't have a good night's sleep and Ruth Tilley's attitude towards Kate Lowe this morning upset me. I took it out on you.'

'You can take it out on me any time you like if you choose the same *modus operandi,*' he said. 'In fact, how about we have dinner tonight and we can pick another fight? Is it your turn to choose or mine?'

'I think it might be your turn,' she said, unable to affect a reproving look in time and smiling at him instead.

He gave her an answering smile and brushed her cheek with the back of his hand. 'Let's keep this out of the corridors, OK? I don't want to have to deal with the speculation right now. There are other pressing matters I have to concentrate on, but that's not to say that during out of working hours we can come to some arrangement that is mutually satisfying.'

She lowered her gaze. 'I understand…'

He tipped up her chin and looked deeply into her eyes. 'I'm not sure you do, Allegra Tallis. I don't think you have a clue about what I'm thinking right now.'

'You don't think I can read your mind?'

His eyes became like dark, unfathomable pools as he held her gaze. 'It's been a long time since I've been in a relationship, for a variety of reasons which I won't go into now. Suffice it to say you don't know me very well. I don't want you to think I'm someone I'm not.'

'We all have baggage,' she said, trying to read his expression, but it was as if a mask had come down over his face, effectively shutting her out.

'Maybe, but being involved with me involves sacrifices most women don't have the fortitude to take. Believe me, I know it from experience.'

'Has someone hurt you in the past?' she asked softly.

'I'm not the broken-hearted sort,' he said. 'I'm

just aware of my own limitations in what I can offer another person in an intimate relationship.'

'You're a nice man, a decent gorgeous man…' She gave him a spontaneous hug, leaning her cheek against his chest where she could feel his heart beating. 'I'm willing to take the chance.'

He put her from him with a gentleness that was girded with firmness, his eyes meeting hers once more. 'We'll see.'

Allegra looked up at him, the shadows in his eyes worrying her. She eased herself away, feeling embarrassed and far too exposed. 'I'm sorry… If you're not interested, just say so. I can handle it.'

'I don't suppose there's any hope of me denying my attraction to you with any efficacy,' he said. 'After all, you have the physical evidence which has been to date both repeatable and provable.'

She smiled crookedly in spite of her inner pain. 'Ever the scientist, aren't you?'

He pulled her close for one last kiss. 'You'd better believe it, baby.'

'I believe it but I still think there's room for the grey areas that science overlooks.'

'I've never said science has all the answers, Allegra. I just don't want you to inadvertently bring disrepute on the unit, especially not now when every calculating eye is on it.'

'You make it sound as if I'm a complete amateur who has no clue what she is doing.'

'*Do* you know what you're doing?'

She frowned at him. 'Of course I do. I want what is best for both the patient and their loved ones.'

'But what if the patient and loved ones have totally different needs, what then?'

'Surely they would want the same things?' she said. 'Life is not a dress rehearsal. This is it. We get one chance at it. Life is precious in all its forms.'

She felt his sigh as if it had happened in her own chest, even though he was now at least half a metre away from her.

'There's a part of me that admires your commitment to what you believe in,' he said heavily. 'But another part—the realistic part—wants to shake you into the real world and show you that what you're searching for doesn't exist.'

'Miracles, you mean?'

'Miracles, fairy dust, aromatherapy—the tools of your moonlighting trade,' he said. 'They just don't bring about the results people are desperate for, and I hate the thought of anyone being fooled into believing they can. It's unspeakably cruel to offer hope when there is none. Lives get destroyed, hanging on the thin thread of a hope that just doesn't exist.'

'I'm not fooling anyone.'

He gave her one of his arched-brow expressions as he opened the door to leave. 'Only yourself, and maybe in the end that is the worst sort of deception of all.'

Allegra sank to the nearest chair as the door closed. She *had* to prove him wrong, but how?

Tommy Lowe was still in the same comatose state when Allegra finished in Theatre to check on him later that day. His BIS monitor scores showed no brain activity and to make matters worse, his temperature had crept up to 38.5.

Keith Lowe came in while she was massaging Tommy's feet, using acupressure to release tension in his little body.

'What are you doing?' Keith gave her a suspicious look, his whole demeanour seeming on edge as he hovered at the side of his son's bed.

'I'm using touch therapy to connect with Tommy,' she explained. 'Children usually have very ticklish feet. It's a way of ramping up the level of sensory input.'

'None of this is working, is it?' Keith said after a long, tense moment.

Allegra stilled her massaging movements to look at him. 'We don't know that yet. We need more time.'

He gave her a defeated look, before shifting his gaze to the monitors and machines that were keeping his son alive. 'If I can't have Tommy back as he was, I don't want him back at all.'

Allegra stared at him in shock. 'You surely can't mean that?'

He met her eyes briefly. 'You don't understand,' he said. 'There's life and there's life.' He rubbed a hand over his face and continued in a tone that sounded empty and defeated. 'I told you yesterday about my family background. My parents were not the emotional, nurturing sort.'

'A lot of parents of your generation weren't,' she offered.

He gave her a brief glance and, shifting his gaze, continued in the same flat, emotionless tone. 'They would have been except for the fact that I had an older sister who was the biggest disappointment of my parents' life. They took their disappointment out on me. If I let them, they would still be doing it.'

Allegra sat very still, a sudden chill travelling down the length of her spine. 'What happened?'

'My older sister had a severe form of autism,' he said, looking down at his hands. 'She was diagnosed far too late to do anything to help her. It ruined my parents' lives, so in a way I can't really blame them for how they reacted to me. I guess it was a combination of guilt and frustration, which they could hardly take out on her so they chose me instead.'

'I'm so sorry. It must have been very difficult for you.'

'Yes…yes, it was…'

'What about your other sister, Serena?' she asked gently. 'Were your parents hard on her as well?'

He met her eyes for a moment before turning away. 'Yes…yes, it was difficult…for both of us.' He released a heavy breath and went on, 'I simply can't bear the thought of my son having a major disability of any sort. Not after what I've been through. I'd would rather he died now.'

'What eventually happened to your older sister?'

'She died of pneumonia at the age of sixteen,' he said. 'I can still see the relief on my parents' faces. I can't help thinking they paid the doctor not to treat her appropriately.'

Allegra felt an upswell of emotion fill her chest until she could hardly breathe with comfort.

'Tommy might not have any form of brain damage at all,' she said, dredging up the last of her hope to convince herself, even as she wanted to convince Tommy's father.

Keith turned to look at her. 'It's a risk I can't afford to take. Not after what I've been through with my sister and my parents. I personally witnessed the damage of what a needy child can do.' He looked down at his hands once more. 'I'm in a new relationship. My…partner would never cope with Tommy if he was…damaged in any way.'

'Don't rush into this,' Allegra pleaded. 'Tommy is a child with his whole life ahead of him.'

'But what sort of life are we talking about?'

Allegra tried not to be put off by the similarity to Joel's words the night before. 'Tommy could make a full recovery. I really believe that,' she said, mentally crossing her fingers.

'That's not what the neurosurgeon intimated,' he said.

'Mr Pardle is a brilliant neurosurgeon, but over the course of his long career he has seen too much to be able to offer hope in cases like this. He's lost children of Tommy's age and condition before and, believe me, it takes its toll, but that's not to say Tommy can't prove everyone wrong.'

Keith got to his feet, his movements slow and tired as if he'd reached the very end of his tether. 'I don't really care what happens with my wife but I want my son to die with dignity. I don't want him to suffer for months on end. I would like his life to count for something.' He scraped a hand through his hair, which did nothing to bring any sort of order to its already haphazard arrangement on his head before he continued, 'Tommy and I discussed this once not that long ago. When the time comes, I want his organs to be donated to give life to others. It's what he would have wanted.'

'You don't have to decide anything like that at this stage,' she said. 'There's still a chance he will wake up.'

'It's a slim chance, though, isn't it?' he asked, for once meeting her gaze directly.

She rolled her lips together, searching for a moment for the right words to say to offer him hope. 'It's slim but not impossible.'

'You're the only one who thinks it's possible. Everyone else I've spoken to has given me a thin slice of hope tempered with the reality of a life blighted by impairment.'

'It might not be anything like that...'

'I can't take the risk,' he said, 'For Tommy's

sake.' He looked down at the small frail figure lying connected to the numerous machines hissing and groaning and pumping in the background, each one keeping the child's life suspended in an indefinable place that had no real future and a past that was all too short.

Seven years.

It had taken Allegra longer to get her qualifications.

'I may not be a great father, according to the rules of the current times, but one thing I know for certain is that Tommy wouldn't want to live half a life,' Keith said. 'I would be an even worse father to stand by and let his life be reduced to that.'

'Please, give me some time with him,' she begged. 'No matter what the other specialists say, please, don't give up until I've exhausted every possible avenue. Please, Mr Lowe…Keith… He's your son, your only child. Surely you owe him this one last chance at life?'

Tears sprang into Keith's eyes and he brushed at them impatiently, clearly embarrassed by this momentary lapse. 'I'm not sure I can do this… It's too risky…'

'What about your sister?' she asked. 'Would she be willing to help me? I can't always do this on my own, I often have to rely on relatives to pitch in.'

His eyes shifted away again. 'I'm not sure my sister is the right person…'

'But your wife asked for her several times during the night,' Allegra informed him.

He looked across at her, surprise evident in his expression. 'Are you sure?'

'Yes, I heard it from one of the nurses and then I heard it myself when I was in her room. She definitely said your sister's name as well as Tommy's. Are they particularly close?'

His eyes fell away from hers. 'I'm afraid Kate hasn't let anyone close to her for years…'

'Depression is a distressing condition for the sufferer and all those in close contact,' Allegra said, recalling her conversation with Judy earlier. 'But perhaps Kate has remembered your sister's past kindness. It happens in cases like this. The most insignificant act of charity can be imprinted on the brain in such a way that when the chips are down, the one person who has stood by is remembered.'

'My wife is not close to anyone,' he said. 'She had a falling-out with her family well before we were married. Her parents haven't even met Tommy. They live in Western Australia. The last we heard it was Fremantle, but they could very well have moved by now. Kate has a sister somewhere…last time I heard she was living in a remote part of a developing country. She's a missionary, but as far as Christian charity goes, it apparently doesn't stretch as far as this.'

'Is there any way of contacting Kate's parents and sister?'

His eyes were cold and distant as they met hers. 'Why would I bother? In many ways they are the reason Kate and I came unstuck. When I married her I thought I could help her overcome her past, but in time I realised it was beyond me. Kate suffered some sort of abuse as a child, she has never said exactly what, but her frequent episodes of depression seem to indicate it was serious.'

So you bailed out when things got tough? Allegra was too professional to say the words out loud, although she dearly longed to, but Keith must have sensed something for he said without apology, 'I have met someone else. She is everything my wife is not. She is confident, assured, going somewhere and determined. She is an extrovert and meets my needs in a way Kate has never done.' He paused, almost guiltily. 'Look, Dr Tallis, I've spent close to ten years propping my wife up with every means available. She's been in and out of clinics and I can no longer carry on supporting her. I want a life of my own without the burden of a partner who is bordering on the psychotic most of the time.'

'But what about your son?'

His eyes fell away from hers again. 'My son is not likely to survive…I know that. I guess I've known it from the first moment. I'm simply doing my best to prepare myself for the inevitable.'

'So you're giving up, just like that?'

'You would do the same if you were in my situation,' he said. 'Most people would.'

'That's not true,' she protested. 'Just because you think something is too tough to face doesn't mean others don't have the courage to face what life dishes up.'

'Maybe life hasn't dished up something you have been thrown by, but you just wait until it does. You might think differently then.'

'Tommy deserves a life,' she said. 'At this moment you are the person who holds that life in your hands. Don't throw it away because of the fear of the unknown. Mr Pardle's and Dr Addison's opinions need to be taken into account, but you have the final say. Please, don't forget that. Don't let their pessimism sway you. They have seen brain damage in all its forms and to a lesser degree so have I, but I have also seen lost opportunities, lives cut short that might have been rehabilitated if given a chance.'

'I can't play Russian roulette with my son's life,' he said. 'I have personally seen the damage of an extremely needy child, how it erodes the very essence of a person's life. I know this is probably a shocking statement for you to hear, but let me tell you there are worse things than the death of a child. Much, much worse.'

Allegra watched as he moved away from his son's bedside, barely sparing a glance at the tiny body on the bed as he twitched aside the curtains and left.

CHAPTER THIRTEEN

ALLEGRA was in the office in ICTU, hunting through the phone book for Serena Fairbright's phone number, when Joel came in.

'Are we still on for tonight?' he asked, his glance going to the f section of the phone book open in front of her. 'Who are you looking for?'

'Tommy's aunt,' she said, running her index finger down the seemingly endless list. 'I wonder what her husband's name is. It would make this a whole lot easier.'

'She might be divorced,' he suggested, looking over her shoulder, his aftershave, in spite of a full day at work, still lingering on him, instantly stirring her senses into overdrive. She disguised her reaction by peering even closer at the fine print, but it became blurred and unreadable.

'Why didn't you ask Keith Lowe for her number when he was in?' he asked. 'I just saw him a few moments ago in the car park, not to speak to, but if he was just here you could have saved yourself the trouble of trawling the phone book, especially if you don't know which suburb the woman lives in.'

She blew out a tiny frustrated breath as she leaned back in her chair. 'Mr Lowe's not the most co-operative person. He doesn't think his sister is going to be much help, but Kate Lowe has said Serena's name several times now, almost as many times as she's said Tommy's.' She closed the phone book in defeat. 'She must have an unlisted number.'

'What did you have in mind for her to do?'

Allegra hunted his face for any sign of ridicule but she was pleasantly surprised by the absence of any such thing. Instead, she saw concern in his dark brown eyes as they held hers.

'I'm not sure…' she confessed, gnawing at her bottom lip for a moment. 'I thought I'd just ask her to come in and sit by Kate's bed and talk to her, you know, like any good friend would do.'

'You're assuming they are good friends,' he said, yet again demonstrating his penchant for solid testable evidence.

'They must have some sort of relationship,' Allegra pointed out. 'She's Kate's sister-in-law and therefore Tommy's aunt. She's visited him at least three times.'

'But not Kate.'

'No…'

'Family relationships can be tricky, especially after what happened in this case. Have you met this woman—the aunt?'

'A couple of times.'

'And?'

'Well, for one thing, you can definitely see they came from the same nest. Mr Lowe told me a little of their background. It was quite tragic so I guess that's why he comes across as so emotionally distant. She's just as bad. Affection was in short supply in their childhood. God knows how they survived it.'

Joel perched on the edge of the desk, his long thighs close to her chest where she sat in the chair. 'What happened?'

She met his eyes. 'He had a sister with autism, a severe form apparently, the eventual diagnosis too late to help. The parents weren't able to cope and took it out on Keith—his sister Serena, too, I suppose—but I get the feeling he copped the brunt of it for some reason.'

Joel's gaze shifted from hers as he looked at the closed phone book in front of her. 'That's tough. No wonder he's so uncomfortable with illness and hospitals. It must bring back some pretty distressing memories.'

'Yes…' She pushed back her chair and stood up and stretched, visibly wincing as a muscle protested in her back.

He sent her a teasing look. 'Maybe I should cancel dinner and book you in for a massage instead. But, then, I seem to recall you telling me you would need to be comatose to allow me to do it, or words to that effect.'

She gave him a playful poke in the ribs. 'If I don't get something to eat and drink in the next hour, I *am* going to be comatose, and it would take a whole lot more than a massage to wake me.'

'Ah, but you haven't yet experienced the magic of my touch,' he said. 'Or at least not on the whole of your body.'

Her eyes met his and she felt a sensation pass through her that felt like a surge of electricity at the thought of his hands moving all over her already tingling flesh. She could well imagine his touch would do more than wake her from a deeply unconscious state. In some ways she felt he had already done so. For years she had avoided the emotional intensity of an intimate relationship and yet his very first kiss had brought her to full and vibrant life.

'Come on,' he said, as he began to lead her out of the office. 'We'd better get out of here before someone needs us. I've had a fifteen-hour day as it is.'

'Only fifteen?' She glanced up at him playfully. 'What are you doing, slowing down or something?'

He grinned as he waited for her to pass him in the unit doorway. 'You're a fine one to talk, young lady. I will have to think of a way to make you forget about work for a while. Good food, good wine and something else.'

'A good movie?'

He tapped her on the end of her uptilted nose, his dark eyes smouldering with promise. 'You'll just have to wait and see.'

The restaurant Joel had booked was in the Southgate complex, a strip of shops, bars and restaurants along the Yarra River, interspersed with hotels, galleries and the world-renowned Crown Casino situated at the far southern end. The Italian restaurant he'd chosen was exclusive and intimate, and they were soon led to a table overlooking the river where the late evening summer sunshine was shimmering on the surface of the notoriously murky-looking water.

Joel caught her looking down at the river and smiled. 'It's not exactly tempting in terms of taking a dip, is it?'

She returned his smile. 'I've been in many times. I was a rower for my school team. Many times on frosty mornings I rowed up and down further along from here.'

'I'm impressed,' he said, leaning back as the waiter handed him a menu and the wine list. 'Do you still row?'

'On the rare occasions my nagging conscience compels me to go to the gym. I do the token thing with the rowing machine, feeling a fool for breaking out in a sweat after three minutes.'

He gave a soft chuckle of laughter. 'I know the feeling. I haven't been near a gym for ages.'

'How do you keep so…so pumped?' she asked.

'Pumped?'

'You know…' She gave him a little embarrassed glance, trying not to let her gaze linger too long on the broad muscles of his shoulders clearly visible through his shirt. 'You've got a well-defined body. You must do something to keep it in shape.'

'I run a bit, I also push a few weights around the house, more to move them out of the way when I haul the vacuum cleaner around.'

Allegra couldn't hold back a gurgle of amusement. 'There must be thousands of homes out there with unused gym equipment gathering dust and cobwebs. I hired a treadmill once but in the end I used it as a clothes horse. I really missed it when the contract ran out.'

His mouth softened in a smile, his eyes warm as they meshed with hers. 'What do you think about the hospital installing a gym for the staff?' he asked.

Her hand stalled as she reached for her water glass. 'Wow, you really are an ideas man, aren't you?'

'Seriously, though, Allegra,' he said, leaning his forearms on the table, 'what do you think? Would you, for instance, use it if it was available?'

She thought about it for a moment. 'I guess it would be better having it on site rather than going home exhausted from work and trying to summon up the energy to go out again to a local gym.'

'And it would encourage a community atmosphere among the staff,' he said. 'I know it's not an original idea—there are other hospitals with gyms—but I thought it would be a way of building a better social network. I get the feeling there are warring factions all over the place at Melbourne Memorial.'

'Yes, that's true, but only because, like every other public hospital, everyone is overworked and stressed. The new development came at a high price for other specialties.'

'I am very much aware of that, and that's why I want to do everything within my power to make this work.'

'Even if it means I don't get to achieve the goals of my project?'

He lifted his eyes from the menu he'd been looking at to connect with hers. 'Let's not fight tonight, Allegra. I'm tired and so are you. We'd end up saying things we don't mean and ruining what could prove to be a really nice evening.'

'I know, but I can't help feeling the pressure of time running out. I want more time to work with Tommy Lowe.'

His eyes clashed with hers. 'Is that why you agreed to come out with me, to try and convince me to change my mind?'

Allegra didn't like the accusing edge to his tone. 'Is it so much to ask? He's a small child. What are a few more weeks? Surely you can allow me that to work a little longer with him?'

Joel put down the menu as if the thought of food was suddenly nauseating. 'Drop it, Allegra. I don't wish to discuss work this evening.'

Something about the implacability of his expression made her back down. It wasn't something she was used to doing, but she recognised the pressure they had both been under and, like him, wanted to enjoy the evening for what it was. Heaven knew, they both deserved a break. It had been a hell of a week so far and wasn't over yet.

'All right,' she said, picking up her menu and burying her nose in it.

Joel stole a glance at her, inwardly grimacing at the way her eyes were doing their best to avoid his. He knew how passionate she was about the Lowe boy and privately he admired and loved her for it. He'd seen the same passion so many times, and yet from his personal experience he couldn't quite allow her free rein. He knew the other side and it wasn't pretty. He admired her for believing in miracles, he had believed in them himself once. So, too, had his parents until the brutal blow of reality had laid its heavy weight on their shoulders. He felt the crushing burden of it even now. He imagined his parents just kilometres away, locked in a prison of suffering that had no key to freedom.

'Guess what?' Allegra said, jolting him out of his tortured reverie. 'They have pizza on the menu.'

He gave her a twisted smile. 'No kidding?'

She showed him the place on her menu. 'See.

Pizza. I know it's in garlic or herb bread form, but pizza is pizza.'

'Let's have a look at the wine list,' he said, reaching for it and giving it a quick perusal. 'I think we should have the most expensive one to compensate.'

'But I feel like pizza bread tonight,' she said. 'Would you mind?'

He rolled his eyes. 'I wish there was a manual issued with every woman, just like a car, so a guy has a chance to figure out how to work her out.'

'I'm not that complicated,' she defended herself, with a little smile.

'Yes, you are.'

'No more than you.'

'What makes you say that?' he asked, pretending an avid interest in the wine list.

'You have an atmosphere of pain around you.'

He didn't bother lifting his head from the wine list. 'So we're back to reading auras, are we?'

'I have never said at any point that I was into reading auras,' she said. 'I don't even know what exactly what the word means. But I do know that every person sends off body language and I am very familiar with reading those signals.'

'So what does my body language reveal to you

apart from an atmosphere of pain, which could simply mean I have a headache or a stomach upset?'

'Are you unwell?'

He raised his eyes to hers. 'I'm a doctor, for God's sake. Do you think I wouldn't be able to tell if I was sick or not?'

'Doctors make terrible self-diagnosticians and even worse patients,' she pointed out rationally. 'We all kid ourselves that illness can't happen to us. We develop a sense of invulnerability. Then we overlook the most obvious signs in ourselves when disease does occur, and try to just carry on while everyone around us is telling we look grey and sickly.'

'I can assure you I am very well at present. I am, however, tired and have a tendency for tension headaches from time to time, but apart from that I enjoy robust health, so there goes your body language theory.'

'I could give you a massage to ease the tension in your neck,' she offered.

His dark eyes connected with hers. 'Only if you promise to work your way down to where the real tension is building every minute I sit looking at you.'

Allegra felt the full force of his sexual invitation, as if he had reached right across the table and touched her where she most wanted to be touched.

A shiver of anticipation ran the length of her spine, lingering among the fine hairs at the back of her neck until she could barely sit still in her seat. She was incredibly conscious of his long muscled thighs just centimetres from her own. And she knew if she so much as stretched her legs, she would encounter them. The temptation to do so was almost overwhelming.

'Is a relationship between us advisable?' she asked, more out of a need to fill the suddenly throbbing silence than any real need to know. She already knew the answer. It was asking for trouble to get involved with a man who held so much of himself aloof. Her mother would be appalled. Her father would immediately try and diagnose some sort of personality disorder, no doubt warning her about becoming involved with a man who seemed to have 'Keep Away' invisibly printed on his forehead.

'Probably not, but we can keep it private,' he said. 'At least for the time being.'

'Great,' she said with heavy sarcasm. 'I finally find a man I admire and respect, and he wants me to keep our relationship quiet. Some girls have all the luck.'

He reached for her hand across the table, linking his long fingers with hers. 'Listen, Allegra. You're a beautiful person. I'm seriously attracted to you, probably more attracted to you than I have been to anyone in the last decade. But I can't make you promises that this will last for ever. I'm not planning to head down the marriage-and-kids track. I think you need to know that from the outset. If you want an affair with me, I am more than willing to commit to that for however long it works for us, but as to a house in the suburbs and a couple of kids and a car pool routine—forget it. It's just not me.'

Allegra felt as if someone had ripped her heart from her chest. She felt empty and hollow inside, bleeding and raw, torn apart with the pain of making a choice that she knew would only cause her more suffering in the end.

In spite of her parents' open relationship, the one thing she had longed for all her life had been a wedding with all the regalia. It was practically every girl's dream to be a princess for a day, and she was no different. She wanted kids, two at least, and a dog, maybe even a cat, one of those big fluffy ones that left long hairs on the couch. She wanted runny noses and sleepless nights; she wanted her own Tommy, a little boy with the world in front of him. She wanted a princess, just like Alice Greeson had been for her parents. She wanted it all. And most of all she wanted Joel Addison—but he came with conditions, conditions she wasn't sure she could cope with.

'This is a tough decision to make.' She tried her best to sound light-hearted, even as her very bones ached and creaked with disappointment.

'I would have thought someone with your sort of progressive background would have jumped at the chance of a no-strings affair,' he said.

'Yeah, well, strange as it may seem, my parents' example has had a sort of reverse psychology effect. I can think of nothing better than settling down with someone, building a life and family with them and working for common goals, just like your parents have. You said they've been married for close to thirty-five years. Doesn't that prove that long-term relationships do sometimes work?'

Joel was relieved with the waiter arrived to take their order. It saved him having to tell Allegra his parents had lived in misery for the majority of that time, linked together by tragedy. He gave the waiter his order after Allegra gave hers and deftly changed the subject, inwardly sighing with relief when she spoke animatedly of a movie she'd seen recently. Fortunately it was one he'd seen as well, which meant he could continue to steer the subject away from his personal life—that had to remain private for as long as he could keep it that way.

CHAPTER FOURTEEN

AFTER their meal was over they took a leisurely walk along the waterfront, stopping to listen to a particularly entertaining busker who was playing a banjo with great enthusiasm and mediocre skill. The night was still warm but a light breeze had taken the sting out of the February heat and the pitch out of the banjo. Allegra found it a slightly strange but delightful experience, walking hand in hand with Joel, their footsteps in time, although she was very much aware he'd shortened his long stride to accommodate her shorter one.

They hadn't spoken much during the rest of their dinner together. Allegra had sensed that she had stepped a little too close in remarking on the pain she felt surrounded him. She imagined it had something to do with his time in the Middle East. One of her former colleagues, who now worked in Brisbane, had spent six months in a war-torn town and had suffered post-traumatic stress pretty much indefinitely afterwards. Even the mention of the country was enough to stimulate painful memories.

Joel hadn't returned to the subject of their relationship either, and she hadn't pressed him on it, somehow sensing he was keen to take things one day at a time. She knew that was more or less the pattern of modern relationships these days. The term used to describe such arrangements was a crude one, but essentially boiled down to having a no-strings sexual partner on call whenever you wanted company. It wasn't what she wanted but she did want Joel, and if that was the only way to have him then she would settle for that and try to be content with it.

'I should get you home,' Joel said, once they had walked back the way they had come. 'It's getting late and we've both been up for far too many hours.'

'Yes, I guess you're right. Are you on early tomorrow?'

He glanced at his watch. 'It already is tomorrow.'

Allegra looked at her own watch and groaned. 'How could it possibly be one a.m.? Last time I checked it was nine-thirty.'

He linked his arm through hers and led her towards the rear of the boardwalk where his car was parked. 'You know what they say—time seems to fly when you're having fun.'

'Did you have fun tonight?' she asked, looking up at him.

He held her gaze for a long moment. 'Yes.'

She slipped into his car and breathed in the scent of leather and his aftershave, wondering if he would take their relationship to the next level tonight. Her body came alive at the thought of being possessed by him, all her nerves leaping inside her skin, the blood in her veins beginning to pump with increasing fervour.

Joel walked her to her door and when she asked him to come in for coffee she knew the only thing that was going to be boiling was the passion she could see reflected in his eyes as they locked down on hers as the door closed after they'd entered her apartment.

'This is the part when you say "Thanks for a lovely evening" and send me on my way,' he said, looking down at her mouth.

'OK… I'll give it a shot,' she said, moistening her lips. 'Thanks for a lovely evening. There, how did I do?'

He pulled her closer until their bodies were touching all the way down. 'That was good. Now this is the part where I give you a goodnight kiss.'

'Sounds good,' she said, watching in mesmerised fascination as his mouth came down and covered hers. It was a very soft brushing of lips, stirring every single sensitive nerve of her mouth into a wanton craving for more.

He lifted his head and stared down into her eyes. 'How was that?'

'Not bad. So what happens now?'

'Well, theoretically I should get my butt out of here within the next four or five seconds, otherwise I suspect the sleep we both need is going to be temporarily postponed.'

Allegra stood silently before him, her body pressed against his as she mentally counted the seconds, one million and one, one million and two, one million and three, one million and four, one million and…

Joel's head came back down and a deep groan escaped from his mouth just as it connected with hers again, this time in a searing kiss of out-of-control desire, his arms wrapping around her tightly. His tongue entering her mouth set off a fiery explosion of need throughout her body.

Somehow through a series of stumbles and furniture-knocking on the way, they made it to her bedroom, falling in a tangle of limbs on her bed.

His weight on her was a blessed burden, their clothes a barrier that was soon dispensed with in hurried, almost frenzied movements of hands and fingers. Hands dealt with buttons and zips, shoes thudded to the floor, along with the softer landing of clothing being tossed aside in order to gain access to naked skin.

Allegra had never felt so swept away by desire before. She'd had two lovers previously but she could not recall ever feeling this incredible wave of longing with either of them. It made her feel as if her whole body was collapsing with it, the hollow emptiness that longed to be filled gnawing at her like a savage hunger she'd never experienced before. She had no control over it. Her body ached from head to toe with the need to feel Joel inside her. She didn't care that they hardly knew each other, she didn't care that he was the one person in the way of her achieving her goal with her project—all that mattered right now was his touch, the heat of his mouth, the raspy sexiness of his tongue and his hardened arousal probing her in its quest for the liquid warm sheath of her body.

His mouth found her naked breast and sucked on it hard. She arched her back in pleasure as his tongue rolled over her engorged nipple, the feel of his moist heat almost too much for her to bear. She whimpered in rapture as he moved to her other breast, one of his hands splayed over her flat abdomen, his long fingers reaching for the short, neatly cropped curls that housed her femininity.

'Oh, my *God*…' she gasped as she tried to hold back, but there was no way of stopping the storm of feeling that crashed over her as he continued his caressing movements against her. She felt herself lift off and soar, floating for a moment before tumbling down in a splintering of sensation that felt as if the skin of her scalp was lifting with the sheer ecstasy of it all.

'You are so very responsive,' he said against her mouth.

'Not usually…' She tried to get her breathing under some measure of control. She stretched like a languorous cat who had over-indulged on the richest cream.

'You're not getting sleepy on me, are you?' he asked, tipping up her chin to look deeply into her passion-slaked eyes.

'No,' she said, smiling as she traced a fingertip over his upper lip. 'It's your turn, I believe.'

'Only if you've got a condom handy,' he said

with a rueful grimace. 'I've somehow got out of the habit of carrying them.'

Her eyes went wide and her chest slammed with panic. 'You've been having unsafe sex?'

He shook his head. 'I've been celibate for eighteen months. Not by choice, more by circumstance.'

'Well, thank God for friends like Kellie Wilton,' she said, as she rolled towards her bedside table and opened the top drawer. She took out a packet of condoms and dangled them in front of him. 'What do you think?'

He took one from the pack, his dark eyes alight with purpose. 'I think you're right—it's my turn.'

Allegra sighed raggedly as he possessed her, his body rocking with building momentum, taking hers along with it in a rush of feeling that gave her no choice but to respond. He carried her along on the tide of pleasure she could hear in each of his deep, rumbling groans. She felt the delicious pause that signalled he was hovering precariously on the edge, his whole body tensing momentarily before he fell forward with a thrusting plunge into paradise, his raw groan of release triggering a wave of pleasure through her as his body jerked urgently against hers until, finally spent, he went limp in her arms in a way she found touchingly vulnerable and trusting—again, a new experience for her.

'How many condoms did your friend give you?' Joel asked, after they had come back to earth a few moments later.

Allegra propped herself up on her elbows and gave him a sultry smile. 'Enough to wear out the average man.'

His dark eyes flickered with unmistakable desire as he pressed her back down on the bed. 'Perhaps I should have warned you earlier—I'm not the average man.'

Allegra smiled as he settled himself between her thighs. 'I knew that.'

'Was it my aura that gave me away?' he asked with a teasing smile. When she smiled up at him he felt himself go over the edge with a plummet of feeling that made him forget about everything but the mind-blowing experience of being with a woman he was rapidly falling in love with.

That in itself was a first—allowing himself to feel an emotion so deep and consuming that it threatened the high wall of resistance he had constructed around himself for most of his life. Allegra Tallis with her way-out ideas but deeply caring nature had, almost from the moment he had met her, been systematically demolishing his barriers, brick by brick, until if he wasn't careful she would finally see him for who he really was.

He had nothing to offer her.

What woman would commit to his responsibilities once his parents could no longer cope? They were heading inexorably that way as each day passed. The brief phone conversation he'd had with his mother the previous day had confirmed yet again that time was running out. He had sensed the desperation in her voice and yet again the craggy fingers of guilt had clawed and scraped at his insides.

Allegra deserved much more than he could give her. Her life would become burdened as his had become when fate had chosen its victim, leaving Joel with the crushing weight of survivor guilt that would never go away, no matter how hard he tried to ignore it or rationalise it away. Even thousands of kilometres had done nothing to separate him from it.

Allegra wriggled back up to snuggle close and a clamp tightened around his heart. He placed his arms around her and held her close, one of his hands going to the back of her head, his fingers stroking through the silky strands of her hair.

There was so much he wanted to say but the

words were locked in his throat. The irony wasn't lost on him.

After all, wasn't Jared, his identical twin, exactly the same?

CHAPTER FIFTEEN

ALLEGRA woke to the sensation of Joel's mouth pressing a soft kiss to the naked skin of her shoulder. She dragged herself upright, her eyes adjusting to the light from the struggling sunshine at war with some storm clouds that looked very much as if they were going to win in the end.

'I've got to leave,' he said, regret in his tone as he looked down at her.

'What time is it?' She peered at the clock by her bedside but her eyes were sticky and blurry from lack of sleep.

'Five-thirty. I've got to get back to my house and shower and be back at the hospital in time for the intensive care and anaesthetic registrar tutorial.'

'You work too hard.'

He dropped a swift kiss to her soft bow of her mouth. 'So do you. See you at the unit.'

'Joel?'

He turned at her bedroom door to look back at her, his heart squeezing at how adorable she looked all mussed from sleep and sex, her mouth swollen from his kisses and the fragrance of their intimacy lingering in the air between them, linking them in a way he'd never felt before.

He hid his reaction behind an emotionally distant one-word response. 'Yes?'

'I enjoyed last night. I know you're not ready for a long-term commitment but I just want you to know that I really enjoy your company.'

He allowed his guard to slip a fraction as a smile softened his features. 'I enjoyed it, too. But I wonder how long it will be before the whole of Melbourne Memorial is in on our secret relationship?'

'Is that going to be a problem for you?'

'No, but it's going to be a problem for you when I have to review your project.'

Allegra stared at him, wondering what to make of his comment. Had last night meant nothing to him? Would he still—in spite of their relationship—put an end to her study?

'I just want some more time,' she said. 'Surely you owe me that?'

His expression hardened. 'The first thing you

should get straight in your head, Allegra, is that it is always a fatal error to sleep with the enemy.'

'What are you saying, Joel?' she asked. 'That you're my enemy? That what occurred between us last night meant absolutely nothing to you?'

'What I'm saying is that if you think by offering your body as a means to sway me into your way of thinking, you have definitely deluded yourself. My assessment still stands. The decisions I have to make in ICTU have nothing to do with whatever relationship we conduct outside work hours. If I feel it's appropriate to pull the plug on your study or advise either Keith Lowe or whoever else happens to have a relative classified as brain dead, I will make those decisions on professional grounds and stand by them, irrespective of what happens between us privately.'

'Then perhaps it will make things a whole lot less complicated if we put an end to this right now,' she said. 'I can't see the point in having a relationship with someone who is so determined to play God.'

'Fine,' he said. 'I guess I'll have to clock last night up as a one-night stand—my first, in fact. You should feel honoured.'

She clutched the pillow with white-knuckled force to stop herself throwing it at him. 'I don't feel honoured. I feel disgusted.'

'So I guess this is the part where I leave and say thanks for the memories?' he said, unable to remove the mockery from his tone.

She threw off the covers and, wrapping the sheet around herself, stomped over to him and wrenched open her bedroom door, her green gaze glittering up at him with rage. 'No, this is the part where I tell you to go to hell and that I never want to see you again.'

'Which, of course, would work if not for the fact that we still have to work together,' he said in the same mocking tone.

'I don't think that is going to be a problem for too much longer,' she threatened. 'Because if you put a stop to my project, I swear I will resign the very next day.'

'There are plenty of other anaesthetists who will gladly take your place,' he said, knowing it was lie and that no one could ever reproduce her particular mix of skills. What she brought to the unit and indeed to Theatre was clearly going to be hard to replace, but his pride would not allow him to admit it.

'Then go and find one who will work the hours I do and care for people everyone else has given up on,' she threw back, tears spouting from her eyes. She scrubbed at her eyes but it was too late—he'd seen them.

He took a step towards her but she held him off with a raised hand. 'Get out. I mean it, Addison. Get out or I'll call the police and have you physically removed.'

He held her challenging glare for a tense moment before he turned on his heel and left. It was better this way, he consoled himself on his way out to his car. Better to put an end to it now before the hurt became more permanent. But as he drove away the ache inside felt as if it had lodged itself in a place that wasn't going to be so easy to remove.

Maybe it was already too late.

Joel had finished his tutorial and the morning ICTU round when his pager beeped. He unclipped it from his belt and read the message. *Drowning: due in TRU 10 minutes.*

He took a breath to prepare himself. The trauma reception unit, with the intensivists involved as early as possible in the management of incoming trauma, was one of the main advantages of the unit. He'd always maintained that hospital management should be involved in clinical decisions and not become isolated from patients. He had seen the all-too-familiar pattern of decision-making by managers who had lost touch with the real issues of patient care. That's why he had put himself on the standard roster of duty for intensivists and today he happened to be the floor co-ordinator for the whole complex.

He finished the medical entry in the last patient's notes and made his way to Trauma Reception.

As he arrived, an ambulance was backing into the ambulance bay and the TRU consultant, Rod Banks, and his registrar, Justin Denby, were busy setting up bay one with the help of nursing staff.

'Dr Addison,' Rod greeted him quickly. 'The patient's just arrived.'

'Do we have any preliminary details?' Joel asked after he'd replied to the greeting with one of his own.

'A guy in his mid-thirties found floating face down in a swimming pool in Toorak. Apparently has a head injury, unconscious, intubated. That's about it until the ambulance crew fills us in.'

'You'll supervise the resus, then, Rod? I'll lend a hand with Justin,' Joel said.

'I don't mind,' Rod said, 'but why don't you take this one? Justin and I were up half of last night at the resident's dinner—we've both feeling a bit seedy.'

'OK, it looks like we're on, then,' Joel said, as the ambulance crew wheeled in a pallid man, head bandaged, his neck in a cervical collar, intubated and being ventilated by one of the crew.

'Justin, you take over ventilation,' Joel directed. 'Rod, can you supervise the transfer to the trauma bed, check the line and get in another IV, and get off bloods for pathology?'

He turned his attention to the attending nursing staff, issuing directions on removing the patient's overalls and inserting a nasogastric tube. As the nurses cut away the patient's clothing, Joel noticed the logo on the right-hand breast pocket, which seemed to suggest the man was some type of pool maintenance technician. Presumably he had met with some sort of accident, perhaps falling into a pool he was servicing.

He turned to address the ambulance crew. 'Any details on this patient?'

The senior paramedic spoke first. 'We were called by the neighbour next door. She claims she heard some sort of argument going on but she was busy with one of her young kids so didn't go out to investigate. A short time later she came out and looked over the fence and saw this guy face down in the pool. She called out to another neighbour on the other side who was mowing his lawn. He hauled the patient out of the pool while she ran back and phoned the emergency services. When we got there the patient had sputtering respirations, obviously lungs still full of water and a stream of blood from the back of his head. I intubated him and sucked out his lungs as best as I could, put on a hard cervical collar and bandaged his head to control the bleeding. My guess is he's got a fractured skull.'

'What's with the police?' Joel asked, nodding his head to where two officers were standing across the corridor.

'I called them,' the senior paramedic said. 'It's now our standard protocol if there is a potentially fatal trauma. They seemed a bit agitated at the scene. The extent of the head injury doesn't sit well with where he was found.'

Joel made a mental note to confer with the police once he had stabilised the patient.

'Second line's in,' Rod said. 'And the nasogastric's returned about a litre of bile-tinged pool water. This guy didn't go down without a fight. To swallow all that water you'd have to be conscious for a fair while.'

'It doesn't look like an accident,' Joel said. 'The police are interested and the ambos suspect a fractured skull. Can we reassess the primary survey?

Then I want a look at that skull and do the secondary survey.'

Joel replaced his gloves with a clean pair and, adjusting his splash-guard goggles, removed the head bandage from the patient. What he saw was clearly not the result of an accidental poolside slip or fall. The back and the side of the skull were crushed, there was bony crepitus, and obvious cerebrospinal fluid leakage from one ear, as well as renewed bleeding once the pressure from the bandage was removed.

'Hell, what's happened to this guy?' he said, in shock at the extent of injury.

Rod inspected the site and grimaced. 'Doesn't look like a trip on slippery tiles, does it?'

Joel gave him a grim glance before he ensured the head bandage was adequately reapplied. 'No, it does not.' He swivelled to address the nurse. 'Get Neurosurgery on the phone. We need an immediate CAT scan to establish the extent of injury.'

Once the nurse had left to do as he'd instructed, Joel turned back to Rod. 'Let's run through the secondary survey, then I'd better have a word with the police.'

'He's not going to make it, is he?' Rod asked.

'If he does, he might not like what's left of his life,' Joel said, performing a detailed head-to-toe examination of the now stabilised patient. Stripping off his gloves and protective gear, he then made his way over to where the police were waiting to speak to him.

After receiving a brief description of the patient's injuries, the officer in charge of the investigation said, 'We'd like to follow up on this. You said you've ordered blood tests, I assume you have included a drug screen?'

'Yes, it's standard procedure,' Joel said. 'Do you guys have any personal details on this man? His name or relatives who need to be informed of his condition?'

'His name is Terry Fowler,' the second officer informed him. 'He's well known to us, if you know what I mean.'

Joel screwed up his mouth for a moment as he took this in. 'He's got some sort of record?'

'As long as your arm,' the older officer said. 'Looks like someone meant business. He wasn't meant to survive, going by what we saw at the scene.'

'So it's an attempted murder investigation?' Joel queried.

'We're treating it that way for the moment, yes. We're following up on a couple of other leads,' the officer said. 'We'll keep you informed of anything relevant. We've organised a guard. We'll try and keep it quiet. This place has had its share of publicity lately.'

'Have you progressed any further in your enquiries into the attempt on Kate Lowe's life?'

The officers exchanged a brief glance before the senior officer turned back to Joel. 'We've now gone through hours of security tapes filmed on the night in question. The image is not as clear as we'd like, but a man with features remarkably similar to Terry Fowler's was captured on tape entering the hospital during the time frame the attempt on Mrs Lowe's life was made.'

Joel frowned, his brain reeling with possible motives. 'Have you any idea what his connection to Kate Lowe would be?'

'Not as yet but, as we said, we have a few leads we're following up. In the meantime, if you think of anything that might be in any way significant, please contact us.' The officer handed Joel a card. 'And it goes without saying that if Mrs Lowe regains full consciousness, we'd like to be informed immediately.'

'Of course,' Joel said.

'How is the little boy doing?' the younger officer asked. 'I have a son the same age.'

'I've been an intensivist too long to offer hope when there isn't any,' Joel said. 'He's showing no signs of brain activity, which means a decision will have to made soon as to what to do next.'

'How's the father taking things?'

'He's doing his best to resign himself for the worst,' Joel said.

'I'm sure his mistress is offering the best comfort she can under the circumstances,' the junior officer said, receiving a quick reproving frown from his superior.

'Yes, well, that's his business, I suppose,' Joel said. 'His sister has been in a few times, or so I'm told.'

'His sister?' The senior officer's frown deepened.

'Yes, I can't quite recall her name...' Joel wrinkled his brow as he tried to recall the name Allegra had been searching for last night before they'd gone for dinner. 'It started with F—Fair-something, I think.'

'Serena Fairbright,' the officer said.

'Yes, that's it. Fairbright.'

'Thank you, Dr Addison,' the officer said. 'We'd better let you get back to your work.'

Joel stood for a while after the police had driven away, a small frown drawing his brows together.

'Dr Addison?' Rod Banks approached. 'I've just

had news about the head-injury guy. He had an arrest in CT—they'd just got him off the scanner. I don't think there was much Mr Pardle could have done, there was major brain damage under the fractures.'

Joel blew out a breath as he turned to go back inside. 'It's probably just as well.'

'Don't let Allegra Tallis hear you say that,' Rod said, more than a little wryly. 'She's in with little Tommy Lowe right now. Apparently the BIS monitor started showing brain activity last night. Allegra whizzed through here and filled me in on the news some time ago—she's busy arranging a repeat EEG.'

Joel stared at him, hope lifting for a moment then crashing back down in his chest. 'What sort of BIS activity did she mention?'

'Not much apparently, but enough to justify another few extra days of monitoring, she thinks,' Rod answered.

'Has the father been told?'

'According to Allegra, he's on his way in.' Rod hesitated for a moment before adding, 'Sorry we couldn't salvage the Fowler chap. I guess his number was up.'

Joel gave the young man a world-weary glance. 'Believe me, he wouldn't have wanted it any other way.'

CHAPTER SIXTEEN

ALLEGRA had not thought when she'd arrived for work that morning that the ache she had felt in her heart could have been eased in any way, but when she had looked at Tommy's overnight BIS monitor scores her hopes had soared in spite of her fractured relationship with Joel.

Kellie, the medical registrar, went through them with Allegra. 'See there, that's definite cerebral activity—at one point it's as high as eight. It's small but there's been nothing prior to that, and the activity has continued at a lower level since then.'

Allegra knew an eight was not an indication of full recovery, far from it, but it meant Tommy had an intact cerebral cortex, and that was the basis for recovery of consciousness.

'Can I see his obs chart for last night?' she requested.

'Sure, here is the chart from midnight the

previous night,' Kellie said, as she passed across a large sheet with manually entered graphs.

'Look at this, Kellie—at around the same time as the first BIS response, there is a rapid rise in pulse and BP. Like a stress response,' Allegra observed.

'I'd not noticed that.'

'Did Tommy have any visitors last night?' Allegra asked. 'His father or aunt?'

'I don't really know. As far as I've heard, it was fairly quiet. I've only just started my shift. I could check with the nurses. Why, do you think something precipitated this?'

Allegra frowned as she looked back at the printouts. 'It's hard to tell. Nothing I've done so far has stirred him and yet here we have an eight seemingly out of the blue.'

'Yeah, well, you and I know an eight isn't exactly an indication that a rocket scientist is still residing inside that little head,' Kellie said.

Allegra flicked a quick glance in her friend's direction. 'No, but it means he deserves more time.'

'Have you told Joel Addison about this latest development?'

Allegra carefully avoided her friend's eyes. 'No, not yet, but no doubt he will soon hear of it and dismiss it as insignificant.'

'Yes, but the father will be pleased surely? He has the final say.'

'The father gave up hope days ago,' Allegra said. 'He's terrified of being left with a permanently disabled child.'

'I can't say I blame him,' Kellie said. 'Have you ever thought about what sort of life some of our patients go on to live once we patch them up and send them on their way?'

'I had the very same conversation with Joel Addison the other night,' Allegra said. 'But then I think of Alice Greeson's parents, who would have been grateful to have taken their daughter home in whatever state she was in. They would have nursed her lovingly for the rest of her life.'

'But what happens when they get too old to do the care?' Kellie asked. 'It falls on the siblings or other relatives, and that's hardly fair. They have their own lives to live.'

Allegra sighed as she thought about it. 'Yes…I can see it's not exactly a black-and-white issue, but I want to do my best in this case. I feel I owe it to Tommy. His mother is clearly mentally ill. Have you seen the self-mutilation scars on her wrists?'

Kellie nodded. 'Sad, isn't it? I wonder what her story is?'

'Probably abuse of some sort in her childhood,' Allegra said. 'The husband intimated as much. He has also had his fair share apparently, his sister, too.'

'They're very close, aren't they?'

Allegra swung her chair around. 'Who, Serena and Kate?'

'No, Keith and his sister.'

'What do you mean, close?'

Kellie gave a little shrug. 'I don't know…it's just an impression I got. You know that date I had organised with the internet dating agency? Well, we met for drinks and then went to that new swanky restaurant on St Kilda Beach. I saw Keith and his sister at a nearby table. I don't think they recognised me. Besides, they hardly even once looked my way. At first I was a bit surprised that a brother and sister would…you know…act that way. It seemed a little weird, sort of creepy.'

'Weird? In what way?' Allegra could feel a strange chill being to pass over her.

'Well…' Kellie dangled her leg from her position where she was perched on the desk beside Allegra. 'I have three brothers and let me tell you as much I love each of them dearly I would never let any of them hold my hands for ages across a restaurant table, and I certainly would never let them kiss me full on the mouth.' She gave a little grimace.

Allegra stared at her friend for so long without speaking that Kellie gave her a little nudge with her foot. 'Hey, what did I say?'

Allegra got to her feet, the office chair she'd been sitting on rolling backwards to bump against the filing cabinet. 'Excuse me, Kel. I have to see Joel Addison for a minute. Page me if anything else happens with Tommy.'

Kellie turned to watch her leave the unit. 'That girl really needs to get out more,' she said to herself, before sliding off the desk and answering the phone that had just started to ring.

Joel was just coming out of his office when he saw Allegra heading his way. He straightened to his full height, mentally preparing himself for yet another showdown, but to his surprise as she got closer he could see no trace of anger on her beautiful face, but worry instead.

'Can I see you for a minute?' she asked.

'Sure.' He reopened his office door and waited for her to precede him, her perfume filling his nostrils as she moved past. 'What can I do for you?'

'Well, for a start let me assure you this is not one

of those morning-after-the-night-before scenes,' she said turning to face him, her slim hands twisting in front of her. 'Neither am I going to apologise and beg you to reconsider our relationship. As far as I'm concerned, you and I are not going to work. It was a moment of madness to even make an attempt.'

'I agree,' he returned coolly.

Allegra fought down the disappointment his response triggered. Couldn't he have at least shown a little remorse for his part in last night? He had offered her nothing but an affair, and it had hurt her terribly to be considered a temporary option. She knew she deserved better than that and he did, too, but for some reason he wasn't interested in even giving it a chance.

'I heard about the BIS monitor scores on the Lowe boy,' he said into the little silence. 'What was the reading?'

Allegra dearly wished she could tell him fifteen, but there was no point lying when he could just as easily verify the results for himself. 'It was an eight for a brief period last night, and a few low-level traces since,' she said. 'His pulse and blood pressure went up for about twenty minutes around the same time.'

'Can you account for it in any of the things you've been doing with him? I heard you were playing his favourite movie repeatedly. Do you think that had something to do with it?'

'I don't know…' She undid her hands to tuck a strand of her hair behind her ear that had slipped from its restraining clip. 'Kellie Wilton, the medical registrar, is checking with the night staff to see if anyone noticed anything.'

'Did he have any visitors during the night?'

'I'm not sure. I'm waiting for the father to come in to ask him. He doesn't usually come in at night, or at least not for very long.'

'I expect he is too busy with his mistress,' Joel said, echoing the cynical opinion of the police officer he'd spoken to earlier.

'Yes…I suppose you could be right…' She worried her bottom lip for a moment before she went on, 'Joel, have you ever met Keith Lowe's sister?'

'No. Why?'

'I have a funny feeling about her,' she said.

'We're not talking auras here, are we?'

Allegra looked up at him but for once there was no sign of mockery on his face. 'Kellie saw Keith and his sister having dinner in a restaurant a couple of nights ago,' she said. 'She saw them holding hands and kissing in a way that suggested they have a slightly unusual relationship for two people who claim to be siblings.'

Joel listened as intently as he could, his brain shooting off in all directions when Allegra tapped into some of his own lurking suspicions. His conversation with the police had stirred up questions that he would very much like some answers to.

'Each family has its own code of affection.' He did his best to go down the logically sequential route. 'Hugs, kisses, that sort of thing vary between family groups, even between individuals within the one family.'

'Yes, I know that, but remember I told you about Keith Lowe's background? How he had been brought up in an overly strict, punitive way? He spoke openly of the difficulty he had showing affection, and yet Kellie swore she saw him holding his sister's hands for ages and kissing her on the mouth. That doesn't add up, to my way of thinking. Besides, I know you don't give much credence to my reading of body language, but I can't help feeling something is not quite right with those two. I understand how having a relative in ICTU is traumatic and makes people act in unpredictable ways, but Serena Fairbright doesn't seem at all attached to Tommy. She barely spends more than a minute or two by his bedside. She hasn't even brought a special toy or anything to him. I know men sometimes overlook those sorts of things, but women are usually good at that. Look at Jonathon Sprent. He may be a fully grown adult but his mum and his sister brought in his childhood teddy bear and a fluffy one-eared rabbit and propped them by his bedside on the very first day he came in.'

'But you said the abusive background of Keith Lowe and his sister made them wary of showing emotion. It seems reasonable to assume that toys and other sentimental tokens of childhood would not feature highly in their scheme of things.'

'I guess you're right…' Her shoulders sagged. 'I just can't help feeling as if something's wrong here and we're not seeing it.'

'Has Kate Lowe had any other episodes of lucidity?' he asked.

'Yes, but that's what's so confusing. She says Tommy's name and then Serena's soon after. If the family is not close in the normal sense, why would Kate be calling for her son and sister-in-law and not her husband?'

Joel frowned as he took in what she was saying. 'I can see what you mean…it doesn't make a lot of sense. But, then, the marriage was in trouble so it could be that Kate confided in Keith's sister about the difficulties she was having.'

'I find that hard to believe, especially since Keith insisted his wife has no close friends. Not only that, you know as well as I do that blood is thicker than water. Why would Serena side with Kate, the woman who had made her brother turn to another woman in desperation?'

Joel's dark gaze locked with hers. 'But what if Serena is not really Keith's sister?'

Allegra stared at him as the penny dropped with a clang inside her head. 'Oh, my God! *She's* his mistress! No wonder she has no affection for Tommy. I can't believe I didn't figure that out first. It's so obvious when you think about it. They don't really resemble each other in looks, although I know that's not unusual—many siblings don't. I just assumed like everyone else that she was his sister. He introduced her as that, I suppose because he was uncomfortable bringing his mistress in to the unit where his wife's and son's lives were hanging in the balance.'

'What if Serena was the one who tried to get rid of Kate?' he said, confirming Allegra's escalating suspicions.

'You mean with the ventilator?' She frowned as she let the possibility sink in. 'But that was a feat of complicated engineering. Serena doesn't strike me as someone with the sort of mechanical skills to cut and join hoses. For a start she has nails practically longer than chopsticks. I can't imagine her using pliers and pipe joiners.'

'No, but what if she got someone else to do it for her? Someone who did have the necessary skills.'

'Who? I mean... Think about it, Joel. How many people could you ask to do something like that without it coming back to bite you? You'd have to pay them a heap of money and hope they kept quiet. It would be an incredible risk to take.'

'Not if you got rid of them permanently.'

Allegra felt a cold shiver pass through her at his words. 'You mean...*murder* them?'

He gave her a grave nod. 'We had a guy come into TRU this morning. The police were very interested in the case. I've been thinking about it ever since.'

'The drowning with the head injury?' she asked. 'I heard something about it. What, they think it wasn't an accident?'

'The head injury he sustained suggested he was bashed with a heavy object, a crowbar or something like that. He may not have fallen into that pool by accident. Someone wanted him to die then and there, but a neighbour heard something and hauled him out. He died before Anthony could get him to Theatre, not that any operation was going to repair his pulp of a brain.'

'But what has this got to do with the Lowes?'

'Nothing maybe, but, as I said, it got me thinking. The guy who died had a criminal record. One could assume he'd be exactly the type to accept a contract, for the right price. Maybe if what we suspect is true, and Serena is not, in fact, Keith's sister but his mistress, she would have a very good motive to get rid of Kate.'

'Maybe…but I still don't understand why Kate would be calling for Serena, the woman her own husband's having an affair with.'

'It happens all the time, Allegra,' he said. 'A mate of mine found out his best friend had been sleeping with his wife for months. He didn't suspect a thing. They played golf together every weekend, had a beer or two once or twice a week after work, but he never once suspected anything was going on.'

'But aren't you clutching at straws? Anyone could have tampered with Kate's ventilator, or at least someone with a bit of inside knowledge. You said it yourself: emotions run high when a child is involved. That's why I asked you to remove Ruth Tilley from the unit.'

'Ruth Tilley has gone on stress leave as of this morning,' he said. 'I don't for a moment suspect her of tampering with Kate's equipment, but the press attention and the police presence has taken its toll on her. It's taking its toll on all of us.'

'I know what you mean,' she said, rubbing her hands up and down her arms. 'I can't believe this place has turned into such a circus. Working in ICTU is stressful enough, without the pressure of a murder inquiry and constant security checks going on in the background.'

'Tell me something I don't already know,' he said, pinching the bridge of his nose, his eyes squeezing shut momentarily.

Allegra looked at him, her earlier anger melting at the obvious stress he was under. His eyes were tired, probably more bloodshot than hers, and his body looked tense, as if he hadn't allowed himself to relax in days, maybe weeks or even months.

She stepped forward and touched him on the arm. 'Joel…sit down and let me massage your neck and shoulders. It won't take long and it will make all the difference, believe me.'

He opened his eyes and met her concerned gaze.

'It's just a tension headache. I get them all the time. I'll take a couple of paracetamol in a minute. Besides, I'm sure you have better things to do right now.'

She smiled and with one firm hand pushed him down into his chair. 'Close your eyes and think of something pleasant. Let yourself relax for ten minutes while I work some magic on those tight muscles of yours.'

Joel settled into the seat but the only pleasurable thing he could think of was how it had felt to have her in his arms the night before, her body writhing beneath his, pleasuring him in an act that he had felt akin to worship. He hadn't been able to remove the images from his mind, no matter how hard he tried. He had pushed her away, just as he had pushed away every other person who had tried to come close, but she was a little more determined than most, a little more—no, a *lot* more—irresistible than most, and it felt good to let his guard down just for a few minutes.

He rolled his head forward as she worked on his tight shoulders through the cotton of his shirt, but he ached to feel her soft warm fingers on his flesh. As if she had read his mind, she moved her hands to the front of his chest and released and removed his tie before undoing each of his shirt buttons, one by one. He did nothing to stop her. He couldn't. The desire to feel her hands on him was so overpowering it was like a fever in his blood.

Finally his shirt was off and her hands were working on his neck and shoulders in rhythmic soothing movements that relaxed those muscles but set up immediate tension in others. He could feel the deep throb of desire spring to life in his groin but he did his best to ignore it, although it took a huge effort. Her fingers increased their pressure, unlocking the tight golfball-sized knots bunched beneath his skin until he finally felt the tension behind his eyes gradually begin to ease.

'How do you feel?' she asked a few minutes later as she handed him his shirt.

He gave her a grateful glance as he shrugged himself back into his shirt. 'That really helped—thanks.'

'You should have more regular massage. People still think it's a luxury treatment that you have once a year when you're on holidays, but it's much more therapeutic if you have it regularly.'

'Yeah, well, time is always an issue,' he said, reaching for his tie.

She watched as he knotted it and positioned it around his throat, adjusting it into place. It was still slightly skew when he'd finished so she stepped forward and centred it.

Joel looked down at her standing so close, her breasts almost touching his chest, one of her hands flat on his chest, the other still on the knot of his tie.

'Allegra…' His voice came out raspy and rough as his hand moved up to cover hers.

'I should get back to work…' she said softly, her eyes feeling as if they were being lured into the deep dark depths of his.

'Yes…yes, you should…' he said, as one of his hands went to the small of her back and brought her forward until she was touching him thigh to thigh.

Her lips were soft and yielding beneath the hard pressure of his, her breath warm and sweet as it filled his mouth and curled around his tongue as he plunged into her moistness. The rush of desire rose in his blood like a rushing tide, as her body instinctively searched for the heat and possession of his.

The mobile phone on his belt brought him back to earth with a shrill reminder of his responsibilities and the lives that depended on him. But when he released Allegra with a wry apologetic grimace and answered it, it wasn't a life that needed saving from within the hospital at all.

It was a life much closer to home…

CHAPTER SEVENTEEN

'How is he doing?' Joel asked the cardiologist in the cardiac unit.

'Your father's had a small inferior myocardial infarct,' Tim Lockerby informed him. 'I want to keep him in for a few days on a streptokinase infusion, and get angiography organised.'

Joel thanked him and moved to the cubicle where his father lay hooked up to an ECG and pulse oximeter, an IV line and oxygen mask.

As if he sensed his son's presence, Garry Addison opened his eyes and removed his oxygen mask. 'Sorry about this, son. I hate to be causing all this fuss.'

Joel took his father's hand in his and gave it a warm affectionate squeeze, fighting back emotion. 'You silly old goat,' he said gruffly. 'You're not causing any fuss. You'll be on your feet again in a few days.'

His father's eyes shifted to the blue cotton open-weave blanket covering him from the waist down. 'Your mother will need some help. I hate to put this on you but—'

'Don't worry.' Joel's grip on his father's hand tightened reassuringly. 'I'll sort something out with Jared. We all knew it would come to this some time.'

'It will break your mother's heart…'

The irony of his father's words weren't lost on Joel. 'At this point in time it's your heart we have to concentrate on. I'll sort out things with Mum, don't worry. I'll take a couple of days off to organise things.'

'But you've only just started this job,' his father protested. 'We've been so worried about the stress you've been under. You look worn out.'

'Well, you're not looking so great yourself, Dad,' Joel joked. 'I'm fine. In fact, not fifteen minutes ago I had a workplace massage. See how well I'm taking care of myself these days?'

'About time, too,' his father grumbled. 'I hope it was done by a pretty woman. It's been far too long since you've had the touch of a woman to take your mind off work and…home…'

'She wasn't pretty,' Joel said, as his patted his father's leg, 'she was gorgeous.'

'So you're dating her?'

He gave his father a mock reproving look. 'Thirty-four-year-old men should never discuss their private lives with their parents, you know that—it could cause heart strain.'

Garry gave him a weary smile. 'Thirty-four-year-old men shouldn't do a lot of things, but sometimes life doesn't hand you the cards you want.'

'How is Jared handling this?' Joel asked after a tiny pause.

'You know Jared. He doesn't make anything easy…'

Joel gave his father another gentle pat. 'Just concentrate on getting well. I'll deal with Jared and Mum. Leave it to me.'

Allegra rushed up to Joel as he was leaving the hospital. 'Joel, how is your father? Is there anything I can do?'

Joel looked down at her, his chest tightening at what might have been if circumstances had been different. 'No, but thanks anyway. He's had a myocardial infarct and needs angiography. I'm taking a couple of days off to sort some domestic stuff out. My mother needs some help. It will take me a day or two to organise it.'

'What about your twin brother?' she asked. 'Can't he help?'

His eyes shifted from hers as he thrust his hand in his trouser pocket for his car keys. 'My brother is totally useless and has been for most of his life.' He rattled his keys impatiently and she stepped back so he could leave.

She watched him drive off, the squeal of his tyres as they hit the tarmac of the road making her wince. It didn't seem fair that he had to shoulder his father's illness without the support of his brother. What were families for anyway, if not to pull together when things got tough? She didn't have a brother or sister but she knew for certain that if she did, they would be close and supportive because her parents would have done everything in their power to ensure it.

Her pager beeped and she looked down at the message, her heart leaping in hope. It was from Kellie, telling her Kate had just regained consciousness.

Kellie was waiting just outside Kate's cubicle when she arrived. 'She's finally awake. She just opened her eyes and asked for Tommy, clear as a bell. The police want to interview her but I thought you should assess her first before they barrage her with questions. They're waiting over there.' She pointed to two tall detectives lingering near the office.

Allegra opened the door to the isolation room where Kate was being managed, and smiled as she approached her bed. Kate still looked terribly fragile, especially as her bruises from the accident had now turned into a kaleidoscope of colour.

'Hello, Kate, my name is Allegra Tallis,' she said, repeating almost verbatim her previous introduction when she'd first visited Kate while she'd been unconscious. 'I'm an anaesthetist on rotation in ICTU. I've been looking after your son.'

'I want to see him,' Kate said, becoming agitated, tears rolling down her cheeks. 'The other doctor and the nurse keep telling me he's all right, but I need to see him to make sure.'

'That can easily be arranged,' Allegra said. 'He's in the unit, further down. He's still unconscious but I'm hopeful he will wake up soon.'

Kate choked on a sob. 'What happened to us? Why are Tommy and I in hospital?'

Allegra's heart sank at the woman's distressed questions. 'You had a car accident a few days ago, Kate. Do you remember anything at all about it?'

Kate screwed up her face as she tried to recollect,

but it was becoming clear she had no memory at all of that day. She shook her head, wincing at the pain it triggered. 'No…it's blank…. I remember we were at the chalet…Tommy and me…'

'What about Keith? Was he there?'

Kate tried to concentrate, but it looked as if she was having trouble with the details. 'I can't remember. He might have been. I think that was the plan… Tommy and I to drive up first and settle in and Keith was going to join us…' She looked at Allegra, her eyes immeasurably sad. 'We've been having some… trouble… My husband wants a divorce. I was upset… I know I'm not a good wife…I get bouts of depression. I don't blame him for wanting to leave me. But Tommy, it would hurt him so much. I thought…if we could just sort things out…'

'So you don't remember why you got in the car with Tommy?'

'No… No, I can't remember.'

'Kate, I know this is going to be difficult for you, but the police want to speak to you about that day.'

'Police! Why the police?' Kate looked frightened. 'Did I do something wrong? Was the accident my fault? Oh, God! Did someone else die? Did I kill someone? Is that why there was a police guard here when I woke up?'

Allegra stroked the woman's hands soothingly. 'No, no one else was hurt, apart from you and Tommy. It was a single-vehicle accident. Your car went off the road into the river. A car travelling behind you saw it happen. He was the one who rescued you and Tommy.'

Kate's distress was obvious. 'Tommy could have died… My precious baby could have died…'

'But he didn't, Kate. He's alive, I'll arrange for your bed to be wheeled to his cubicle.'

Allegra went to where the police were waiting. 'She's still very fragile and has amnesia. It's not a good idea to press her too hard. If she regains her memory, and in cases like this some people never do, she will be able to cope better with a more intensive interview.'

'Does she know someone tried to turn off her ventilator?' the detective sergeant asked.

'I didn't think it wise to mention it,' Allegra said. 'She has enough to deal with at the moment.'

'We'll be maintaining our close watch over her, especially now she is conscious.'

'I don't believe she tried to commit suicide,' Allegra felt compelled to say. 'But I do believe someone wanted her dead.'

'Murder-suicides make people angry, especially

when young children are victims,' the detective said. 'But in this case I'm inclined to agree with you.'

'Oh, really?' She gave him a surprised look. 'Have you uncovered something in your investigation?'

'Dr Addison, your colleague, ran a drug test on a patient that was brought in earlier this morning.'

'Terry Fowler, the head injury-drowning victim?'

'That's the one,' he said. 'As you know, he subsequently died from his head injury, but the pathology report showed up a cocktail of drugs in his system.'

'I haven't seen the report but can you recall exactly what the drugs were?'

'An antidepressant and a sedative,' he replied, checking his notebook. 'I'm not sure of the actual amounts but paroxetine, codeine and diazepam were definitely present.'

Allegra was getting so used to chills running up and down her spine now that she hardly noticed this one as it occurred. 'That's interesting. That's exactly the same cocktail of drugs found in Kate Lowe's blood.'

The detective frowned. 'I'll have the records correlated immediately. There might be some link between Fowler and Mrs Lowe. I'll get our people onto it straight away.'

Allegra went back to Kate's cubicle and immediately organised for her to be transferred to Tommy's bedside. The police guard accompanied them but he kept at a discreet distance.

Kate's face crumpled when she saw her little boy lying hooked up to the ventilator and monitors, his little chest rising and falling mechanically.

Allegra touched her on the arm. 'Don't let the machines upset you. You were on exactly the same ones and here you are awake and getting better by the minute.'

'But what if he doesn't get better?' Kate turned her agonised face to Allegra. 'Brain injury is serious in anyone, more so in a child. What if he's…permanently damaged?'

Allegra tried to offer the best possible hope. 'We are still not sure how severe his head injury is. We've run some tests, which at this stage are inconclusive.'

'This is all my fault…' Kate said brokenly.

'No, that's not true,' Allegra insisted. 'You didn't do anything to deliberately harm Tommy.'

'If only I could remember…' Kate began pulling at her hair as if it was in the way of her memory.

Allegra looked in horror at the clump of hair that came away from the woman's head. 'Kate, please, don't torture yourself like this. Tommy needs you to be strong right now.' She took

Kate's hands in hers and began to massage them. 'I need you to help me get through to Tommy. I know you can't remember anything about the day of the accident, but can you tell me about Tommy's favourite things? His father told me he loves the Harry Potter movies and books and I've had the DVDs running almost constantly, but what about something else? Can you think of anything that he loves more than anything in the world?'

Kate's face brightened with a glimmer of hope. 'He has a teddy bear. He's had him since he was a baby. It's got a little key in the back that when you wind it up it plays "London Bridge is Falling Down." He never goes anywhere without it. He sleeps with it every night.'

'Have you any idea where is the bear now?'

'I don't know… We took it to the chalet but if we left in the car it might have been with us…'

And lying at the bottom of the river, Allegra thought with a sinking feeling. 'I'll chase it up with the police and SES,' she said. 'They usually remove all personal items and return them to the owners.'

'Dr Tallis,' Kate appealed to her with her big soulful hazel eyes. 'I read of a case not that long ago of a girl in a coma. She was declared brain dead and the machines that were keeping her alive were switched off. That won't happen to Tommy, will it?'

Allegra had never felt so out of her depth in her life. 'Kate.' She took the woman's hands in hers once more. 'I promise you that I will do everything in my power to prevent that happening.'

'I don't care if it turns out that he's…damaged,' Kate said. 'I just want him alive. He's my son… my only baby. I will look after him, no matter what. That's what being a mother is all about. He's all I live for.'

Allegra stood back as the orderlies helped to transfer Kate back to her room. Once she was settled, Allegra left to call the SES team that had retrieved Kate's vehicle. As luck would have it, they had found the teddy bear and the man she spoke to was planning to come to Melbourne for a social event and promised to deliver it personally to the hospital.

The next call Allegra made was to Joel, but she got his answering service on both his home number and his mobile. She left a brief message but as the hours dragged by she ached to see him in person, partly for her own reasons but also to talk about the developments the police had discussed with her.

By sheer chance she ran into Tim Lockerby from

the cardiac unit who she knew was looking after Joel's father.

'Tim? Do you happen to know Joel Addison's parents' home address? I need to see him about something and he's not answering either of his phones.'

'It will be on Mr Addison's file. I'll get the ward clerk to give it to you. I heard you've been dating Joel.'

She frowned. 'Who told you that?'

'His father did,' Tim answered, with a glinting smile. 'He was right chuffed about it. Said it was the first time in years his son had been so taken with a woman.'

'I can't imagine Joel Addison announcing to all and sundry that I was the woman of his dreams,' she said with a cynical twist of her mouth.

'He didn't,' Tim said. 'His father figured it out for himself, as did the rest of the staff in CCU. As soon as Joel mentioned he'd had a workplace massage by a gorgeous woman, it was easy to do the numbers and come up with you.'

'He said I was gorgeous?' She gaped at him incredulously.

'Don't you have mirrors at your place?' Tim teased. 'If I wasn't already married to a beautiful woman, I'd be requesting a workplace massage myself. Joel is a great guy, Allegra. You deserve to have a social life. You work too hard as it is.'

'I know. It's getting to me, believe me,' she said with a rueful look.

'Take care of yourself,' he said. 'You've had a tough time recently. Don't go working yourself into a breakdown.'

'I'm fine, Tim, but thanks for being concerned. I'll just get that address and another fourteen-hour day will be over.'

Tim grinned. 'And another will appear tomorrow morning.'

'Don't remind me,' she growled, and made her way to the ward clerk's desk.

The drive out to Box Hill was interrupted by heavy traffic due to roadworks. The heat of the evening was stifling in spite of her car's air-conditioning. She pulled up in front of a modest single-storey house in a quiet leafy street, turned off the engine and took a minute to look around at the house Joel had spent his childhood in.

She wasn't sure what she'd been expecting but somehow she couldn't help thinking the slightly run-down appearance of the house and garden didn't sit all that well with Joel's position as a highly qualified doctor. But then she remembered his car. It, too, was modest, nothing like some of the flashy sports cars that littered the hospital car park.

She made her way up the concrete path, glancing down at the ramp that led to the front door. She pressed the bell and after a short wait the door opened and a small woman with salt-and-pepper hair and a tired face looked up at her with a tentative smile. 'Hello? Can I help you?'

'Mrs Addison?' Allegra offered her hand. 'I'm Allegra Tallis, a doctor at Melbourne Memorial.'

The woman's face seemed to almost collapse in dread. 'This isn't about Garry, is it?' she asked. 'He's all right, isn't he? I'm just on my way to visit him. Don't tell me something's gone wrong before I could get there to be with him.'

'No, nothing like that. Mr Addison is doing very well. I was talking to his cardiologist not long ago,' Allegra quickly reassured her. 'I'm here to see your son, actually.'

The relief on Joel's mother's face completely transformed her features. She placed a thin hand on her chest as if to settle the flutter of her heart. 'Oh, thank God. You had me worried there for a moment. But I'm afraid Joel's not here right now. He's out with his brother, but I'm sure they won't be too long. They went to the park but should be back soon. You can wait here or, if you like, you could go and meet them there. I have to dash. I haven't had a chance to take my husband's toiletries in to him yet.'

'A walk in the park sounds wonderful,' Allegra said, feeling uncomfortable about waiting in Joel's family home alone.

'It's just at the end of the street,' Mrs Addison said. 'It was nice meeting you. I hope you'll come again when things aren't so…so stressful.'

'I'd like that,' Allegra said with complete sincerity. She felt a warmth coming off Joel's mother that somehow reminded her of her own mother.

The pavement was hot under her feet as she walked to where the park was situated. She could see a group of teenage boys kicking a football about and secretly admired their energy in the cloying heaviness of the humidity that suggested a storm was imminent. Perspiration was already plastering her thin cotton blouse to her back and the tops of her thighs were sticking together uncomfortably.

She followed the path for a bit longer until she saw the unmistakable figure of Joel in the distance. He was pushing a wheelchair, and as he came closer she could see the identical image of him sitting slumped in the chair.

She stood stock still as if suddenly frozen, shock widening her eyes as Joel stopped in front of her. She gave herself a rough mental shake and, shifting her gaze to his level, reached out a hand to Joel's brother.

'Hi, you must be Jared,' she said with a smile. 'I'm Allegra.'

'He can't hear you,' Joel said.

She looked up at Joel in astonishment at his curt, emotionless tone. She turned back to Jared and greeted him again, using sign language, but it was clear he had no understanding. He looked at her, his head wobbling as he tried to focus on her face, a smile momentarily appearing on his mouth.

Allegra bent down and took Jared's limp hand in hers and gave it a gentle squeeze. 'Hi, Jared. I'm sorry you can't hear me, but it's nice to meet you.'

Joel looked down at her squatting in front of his brother, his heart feeling as if it had someone had just put it in a vice. This was another first—no woman had ever greeted his twin as a real person before. This was usually the part where they would shrink back in horror, making some hastily murmured embarrassed comment about having something pressing to go to.

He would never see them again.

No one had ever bent down to Jared's level and looked deeply into the eyes that were like his own and smiled at his brother with respect and compassion instead of pity.

'He can't understand a word you say,' he said. 'He's intellectually disabled. He's in a permanent vegetative state.'

Allegra straightened to meet Joel's eyes. 'That doesn't mean he doesn't deserve respect.'

'He shouldn't be alive.'

She stared at him, open-mouthed. 'How can you say that? He's your brother! Your twin brother!'

'He's ruined my parents' lives. My father wouldn't be in hospital right now if it wasn't for Jared. I know it's not his fault, but every day of their life and mine has been tainted with the pain and grief of looking after him twenty-four hours a day.'

She applied the brake on the wheelchair and, taking Joel's arm, led him a short distance from his brother. 'Life is precious, Joel. Your limbs were wrapped around Jared's in your mother's womb for nine months. How can you possibly wish he wasn't alive?'

'Don't misunderstand me, Allegra. I love my brother but it doesn't change the fact that it's no picnic being responsible for him. I've lived with it all my life, knowing that sooner or later the responsibility was going to be handed to me when it became too much for my parents.'

Allegra stared at the moisture glistening in his eyes, her heart aching for what he must have suffered as a child, seeing his brother, the image of him, locked in a body and mind that was surely one of the worst of all human tragedies—permanent and totally devastating disability.

She stepped forward and placed her hand on Joel's arm. 'Why don't you go and have a long walk or have a coffee somewhere while I take over with Jared? It seems like you could do with a break. You've had so much to deal with, you look exhausted.'

'You'll never be able to manage him. None of your fairy-dust theories are going to work, no matter how hard you try.'

'Please, Joel,' she insisted, trying not to be put off by his hardened tone, recognising how he must hate showing his vulnerability in such a raw way. 'Give me the keys to the house and I'll sit with your brother for a couple of hours.'

He handed her the keys, turned on his heel and walked away without a backward glance. She watched him for a moment or two before Jared began to rock back and forth in his chair in frustration.

'Sorry about that, Jared,' she said, bending down to release the brake before straightening to run her fingers through his thick dark hair that so reminded her of Joel's. 'Your brother needs a break.'

Jared rocked again, one of his hands flying upwards to hit her in a glancing blow on her cheek. She couldn't escape it in time and knew it would give her a spectacular bruise, but as she wheeled his chair back along the path, she reminded herself it was nothing compared to what Joel had done to her heart.

CHAPTER EIGHTEEN

ALLEGRA had seriously underestimated the level of care Joel's brother required. No sooner had she entered the house than he began to wail in distress, his arms flailing about until she had to make a conscious effort to duck out of their way. She considered lifting him out of his chair but while he had nothing of the muscled bulk of Joel, he was still at least twice her weight.

She made him a cool drink and after a few attempts, which involved a change of bib, she managed to get some into his mouth. His gulping swallows tore at her heart, his eyes rolling about as he tried to grasp at her with his twisted hands.

She hunted through the refrigerator for some semblance of a meal, and chatted to him all the while as she made an omelette with softly steamed vegetables, presuming his brain damage made it difficult for him to chew normal food.

She was right, for even though she had prepared a mushy meal, most of it ended up on his chest or on the floor. She reassured herself that his hunger must have been satisfied because he seemed to be content for a while, sitting in his chair, looking at her with vacant eyes.

'I'm in love with your brother,' she said into the silence. 'I think you should know that.'

'Meeting you has answered so many of my questions,' she went on. 'He is terrified of someone ending up with what you have to deal with. I can see that now. This isn't easy for you, is it, Jared? It's not easy for your parents and Joel. I have been so focused on my own goals I haven't considered the other side.' She let out a little sigh and continued, 'I have this little boy in ICTU. His scans show he's brain dead. I guess that's a term that your family is pretty familiar with, although clearly your brain still functions in some areas but not enough to give you the sort of life you deserve. Tommy is a little boy of seven. I guess I hadn't ever considered he could end up living the life you are now forced to live. But your parents love you, so does your brother, otherwise he wouldn't have given up so much to be here with you so your mum could visit your dad.'

Jared's head drooped to one side. Allegra sighed as she got wearily to her feet and turned his chair to look for his bedroom.

If feeding him had been one of her biggest challenges, preparing him for bed surpassed it in spades. He was totally incontinent, which meant she had to deal with the change of a soiled nappy while he protested, his contorted limbs flying about until she was close to tears.

Finally she did what had to be done and dragged him towards the mattress on the floor that was his bed. He fought her for a while but she turned him over onto his stomach and began to massage his tight legs, working her way up from his feet until she got to his lower back. His breathing became relaxed and he gradually drifted off to sleep.

She covered him with a light cotton sheet and sat back on her heels and began to cry, softly and brokenly, her heart breaking for what Joel and his parents had endured for so long.

Joel found her there a short time later, her face pink, her eyes red and swollen as she turned to face him.

He gestured for her to leave the room in case his brother woke up and she followed him with dogged steps, her shoulders at an all-time low.

He took her in his arms, burying his head in her fragrant hair as she sobbed against him.

'I'm so sorry…' she choked. 'I had no idea…'

'Most people don't.'

'I can understand why you're so against my project…'

He hugged her close. 'I wish it could work, Allegra. I would give anything for my brother to have even a fraction of the life I have. I feel guilty that it's him, not me. I've carried that all of my life.'

She eased herself away from him to look up at him. 'What happened?'

'Bacterial meningitis. I was born first. Jared's delivery was delayed. By the time he was born, meningitis had taken hold and fried his brain.' He gave her a rueful grimace. 'If he had been first, I would have been the person you would have spent the last couple of hours with, spoon-feeding.'

Allegra felt his pain as if it were her own. 'I would still have done it, and gladly.'

He smiled down at her, although it was tinged with sadness. 'You know something? I think you are the very first person I have ever felt I could have a relationship with. When you took Jared for the last couple of hours I suddenly realised how much I care for you. But I'm what is known as a package deal. My parents will not be able to cope with Jared's care for much longer. There are limited spaces in care homes for people with his level of disability. There are issues to face.'

'But if we face them together, the burden won't be so heavy. I love you, Joel. I think you know that. I would do anything to help you deal with Jared if it means I can be a part of your life.'

'But there is still an unresolved issue between us.'

Allegra knew what was coming and it was now nowhere near as clear-cut as it had been a few short hours ago. 'Kate Lowe regained consciousness earlier today,' she said. 'She remembers nothing of the accident but she is prepared to have Tommy in whatever state he is.'

'She sounds just like my mother. My parents were advised to let Jared go but Mum wouldn't hear of it. They've both had to deal with that decision ever since.'

'So that's why you are so against coma recovery. You don't want to risk the same situation happening.'

'Can you blame me?'

She saw no point in defending her position. 'No, I can see how you've come to the decisions you have. I would have probably done the same. But I had a friend in medical school—I mentioned her to you previously. She had a break-up with a boyfriend and took an overdose. It was an impulsive knee-jerk reaction. On another day she would never have done it, I know it. She was on a ventilator for ten days and her parents were advised to withdraw life support. I had a feeling it had more to do with the organ donor waiting list at the time than Julie's needs.'

'If she was declared brain dead, there was no point stretching out the agony.'

'There's a part of me that realises that—the scientifically trained part of me. However, another part of me believes in second chances. Julie deserved a second chance, as does Tommy.'

'Even if he ends up like my brother?'

That was one question she was unable to answer. 'It's a risk. Some parents are prepared to take it, others not.'

'Well, I for one can tell you I wish my parents had never taken it, and if you asked them they would answer the same. Don't get me wrong—my parents love my brother, they always have. I am constantly amazed by their continued devotion, but the reality is he should never have been resuscitated. Some lives are just not worth living.'

'I know this is the worst possible time to ask you

this, but will you, please, let me work with Tommy a little longer?'

'You can work with him if you are prepared to accept the responsibility of him turning out like Jared. Can you deal with that?'

'I'm hoping it won't come to that. Now that his mother has regained consciousness, I think there's a chance we can touch Tommy's subconscious in a way his father couldn't.'

'Even though Kate did her best to take her life and that of her son?'

'She didn't attempt suicide,' Allegra said. 'I'm absolutely certain of it. Even the police agree with me.'

'Has there been some new development in the investigation?'

'Yes. You know the drug test you ordered on the guy with the head injury? He had a cocktail of drugs in his system—exactly the same cocktail that was found in Kate's blood.'

Joel frowned as he took Allegra's words in. He had been mulling over the possible connections between the Lowe case and Terry Fowler, but so far hadn't come up with anything. But if the same cocktail of drugs had been in Fowler's blood as Kate's then there had to be someone who was connected in some way to both of them.

'Do you happen to know where Serena Fairbright lives?' he asked.

Allegra shook her head. 'No, but we can always get the police to find out.'

Joel unclipped his mobile from his belt and switched it on.

'No wonder you didn't return my calls,' she said, glancing at his phone as it booted up.

'I wanted to forget about the hospital for a while,' he explained. 'I had other pressing matters on my mind.'

Allegra listened as he called a friend in the police force, who gave him the information he was after within a few minutes. He hung up and met her gaze. 'Guess whose pool Terry Fowler services regularly?' he asked.

It was, after all, surprisingly easy to come up with the answer. 'Serena Fairbright's?'

He gave her a grim nod. 'The police are on their way to interview her now. She is, as we suspected, not Keith Lowe's sister but his mistress.'

'If only Tommy would wake up,' she said. 'Kate remembers nothing of that day, but if Tommy regained consciousness we might get all the puzzles pieces on the table.'

Joel met her eyes, his expression offering no

promise. 'He might never wake up, Allegra. You need to prepare yourself and his parents for that possibility.'

'Kate will never agree to turn off his ventilator, no matter what her husband says.'

'Ultimately the court would have to make the final decision on that.'

'I hope it won't come to that.'

'It might,' he warned. 'This could go on for months.'

'I know, but I'm still hoping for a miracle.'

He shook his head at her but for once there was no trace of mockery in his expression. 'I think that's why I've fallen in love with you,' he said. 'That in itself is a miracle. I've never been in love with anyone before.'

She smiled up at him, her eyes shining with hope and joy. 'Neither have I,' she said, and lifted her mouth to kiss his.

CHAPTER NINETEEN

'ALLEGRA.' Kellie rushed towards her as soon as she arrived at the unit the next morning. 'You have to come and see this!'

'What?'

'It's amazing,' Kellie said. 'Tommy's score's gone up to the maximum.'

'Fifteen?' Allegra gasped.

Kellie nodded excitedly. 'The SES guy you called me about dropped in the teddy bear. He was a little the worse for wear but he seems to have done the job.'

'The teddy bear or the SES guy?' Allegra asked as she matched strides with her friend as they made their way to Tommy's cubicle.

Kellie gave her a sheepish look. 'The SES guy was totally gorgeous. We're meeting up this evening and, yes, he was a little worn, but the teddy bear came in a close second.'

Allegra smiled. 'Has Tommy woken up yet?'

'No, but I reckon if you bring in his mum, he won't take long to do so. Shall I get the order-lies onto it?'

'Yes, you do that. Has Keith been in?'

Kellie shook her head. 'He hasn't been in since Kate woke up. I still can't help feeling he has some-thing to do with all this. The police were looking for him, too.'

Allegra entered Tommy's cubicle and was deeply moved by the actions of the attending nurse who was rewinding the teddy bear as if she had done it many times before. She set it by Tommy's head and stepped back, only then noticing Allegra watching her.

She gave Allegra a little smile of embarrassment. 'I have a daughter the same age.'

'Don't apologise,' Allegra said. 'Kids are kids, no matter who they belong to.'

'He's a darling little thing,' Lucy Piermont said. 'So small, but fighting all the way.'

Allegra felt a rush of warmth towards the nurse and wanted to hug her for her show of support for the little boy that just about everyone had given up on. She had to control her urge to cry. Ever since she had spent the evening with Joel and his twin, she had been feeling incredibly emotional. She couldn't stop thinking about Joel and how he had suffered the guilt of being the healthy twin.

'Hi, Tommy,' she said, to force her thoughts away from such painful territory. 'I've arranged for your mum to come in. She's on her way.'

Tommy suddenly opened his eyes and began to fight against the ventilator. His eyes were wide with panic until he twisted his head and saw his teddy bear next to his head. His struggle lessened and his eyes lost their terrified glaze as the music of his infancy calmed him, as it had no doubt done countless times in the past. His eyelids fluttered closed, his chest rising and falling in time with the ventilator, but Allegra knew the major fight had been won.

She vainly tried to swallow back the rising lump of emotion in her throat but it was beyond controlling. She sat, her tears rolling down unheeded as Tommy's mother was wheeled in.

'Oh, my God!' Kate cried as she saw Allegra's face. 'Is he…dead?'

Allegra stumbled to her feet and wrapped her arms around Kate's frail shoulders. 'No,' she sobbed. 'He's alive. He's alive.'

'You mean he's not brain dead?'

'No.' Allegra lifted herself away, scrubbing at her face, still choking back sobs. 'No one who opens their eyes like that can possibly be declared brain dead. We did it, Kate. You did it. You brought your son back from the brink.'

'No.' Kate was openly crying now. 'You did it by not giving up. My son might have been lying on a cold slab in a morgue by now if it hadn't been for you. I owe you so much.'

'Neither of us did it,' Allegra said, looking at the teddy bear propped beside Tommy's head, still playing its song. 'That's the little guy we have to thank.'

A few hours later Tommy was able to breathe without the ventilator and he gradually filled in the memory blanks his mother hadn't been able to fill.

Serena had arrived at the chalet and introduced herself as a neighbour. His mother, out of politeness, had offered her a drink and he recalled Serena had asked for vodka and orange juice, which she helped his mother prepare. Tommy had sipped at a glass of orange juice Serena had poured for him, but he'd felt uncomfortable with her presence. He left the room for a short time, only to come back when he heard a vicious argument erupting between his mother and Serena. His mother had grasped at Tommy and hurriedly bundled him in the car, and she'd seemed very agitated. He could remember that a few minutes into the journey his mother had seemed unable to control the vehicle. Thankfully he couldn't recall the exact moment they had gone over the edge, but he was in no doubt that his mother had been frightened of the other woman and had wanted to put as much distance between them as possible.

The police interviewed Tommy and a short time later sought out Joel and Allegra to fill them in on the rest of what they had discovered in their investigation.

'Terry Fowler was the pool maintenance guy Mrs Fairbright used occasionally,' the detective in charge of the investigation informed them. 'She offered him a contract on Mrs Lowe's life after she herself was unable to successfully bring about Kate's death via the accident. She had slipped a cocktail of drugs into Kate's drink as well as a triple shot of vodka. Her intention was to get rid of the wife and child. She paid him to sabotage the ventilator that was keeping Mrs Lowe alive.'

'Was Keith Lowe involved in any of this?' Joel asked.

The detective shook his head. 'We've taken a statement from him and his alibi stands up. He appears totally devastated by the news of his mistress's actions. We've charged Mrs Fairbright with murder in the first degree for the death of Mr Fowler. She confessed she drugged him, using the same drugs she'd used in Kate and Tommy Lowe's drinks when she'd gone to the chalet. She also confessed to hitting him from behind with a crowbar and pushing him into the pool. She also faces further charges of attempted murder for her actions in regard to Kate and Tommy.'

'Why did she make an attempt on Mr Fowler's life in her own back yard?' Allegra asked. 'Surely she knew it would point the finger of blame at her.'

'When news got out Kate Lowe was beginning to regain consciousness, Mrs Fairbright panicked. Terry Fowler began to put the pressure on her for more money to keep quiet, and she became desperate.'

'It all seems so unbelievable…' Allegra said, rubbing her arms as if warding off a chill.

Joel stepped closer and, placing an arm around her shoulders, pulled her into his warmth. 'Thank you, Detective Lacey, for filling us in.'

'No problem,' he said with a smile. He shifted his gaze to Allegra and added, 'You did an amazing job with the little boy. It was a stroke of genius, getting his teddy bear to him. Who knows what would have happened if he hadn't woken up?'

Allegra was too choked up to answer but Joel spoke for her, his words making her heart swell until it felt as if it was taking up all the space in her chest. 'She's a wonderful doctor who cares very deeply for patients, no matter what potential they are left with. I have learned a lot by working alongside her and this hospital will go down in the history books as one of the most innovative in the country, not because of me, as I had hoped and planned, but because of a young woman who believes in miracles.'

The detective smiled. 'Someone has to believe in miracles,' he said. 'How else would doctors or cops survive the stress and strain of what we have to face every day?' He shook both their hands and, wishing them well, left a short time later.

Joel turned Allegra in his arms, his eyes warm and melting as he looked down at her. 'You know, I'm really getting into this miracle thing myself.'

She smiled up at him. 'What do you mean?'

'My mother has never quite given up hope that I would one day find someone so perfect for me that it would make me rethink my decision to stay single and unattached all my life. She's been praying for a miracle and now she's finally got it.'

Allegra felt as if her chest was going to burst as

she waited for him to continue. His smile lit his eyes and his body, where it was pressed against hers, told her more than words ever could, but she needed to hear them all the same.

'Allegra Tallis,' he said in a gruff, unashamedly emotional voice, 'will you do me the honour of being my wife? I love you and want nothing more than to spend the rest of my life with you. I want you to have my children, two at least, and maybe we could have a dog, one of those with big muddy paws. What do you say?'

She smiled up at him, her green eyes dancing and shining with joy. 'I'm surprised you even felt the need to ask me that. I would have thought my aura had well and truly given me away.'

He grinned as he brought his mouth down close to hers. 'No,' he said. 'It was this.' And his lips covered hers in a kiss that sealed their love for ever.

MEDICAL ROMANCE™

Large Print

Titles for the next six months…

August

A WIFE AND CHILD TO CHERISH   Caroline Anderson
THE SURGEON'S FAMILY MIRACLE   Marion Lennox
A FAMILY TO COME HOME TO   Josie Metcalfe
THE LONDON CONSULTANT'S RESCUE   Joanna Neil
THE DOCTOR'S BABY SURPRISE   Gill Sanderson
THE SPANISH DOCTOR'S CONVENIENT BRIDE
                                 Meredith Webber

September

A FATHER BEYOND COMPARE   Alison Roberts
AN UNEXPECTED PROPOSAL   Amy Andrews
SHEIKH SURGEON, SURPRISE BRIDE Josie Metcalfe
THE SURGEON'S CHOSEN WIFE   Fiona Lowe
A DOCTOR WORTH WAITING FOR Margaret McDonagh
HER L.A. KNIGHT   Lynne Marshall

October

HIS VERY OWN WIFE AND CHILD Caroline Anderson
THE CONSULTANT'S NEW-FOUND FAMILY Kate Hardy
CITY DOCTOR, COUNTRY BRIDE   Abigail Gordon
THE EMERGENCY DOCTOR'S DAUGHTER Lucy Clark
A CHILD TO CARE FOR   Dianne Drake
HIS PREGNANT NURSE   Laura Iding

MILLS & BOON®

0707 LP 2P P1 Medical

MEDICAL ROMANCE™

Large Print

November

A BRIDE FOR GLENMORE	Sarah Morgan
A MARRIAGE MEANT TO BE	Josie Metcalfe
DR CONSTANTINE'S BRIDE	Jennifer Taylor
HIS RUNAWAY NURSE	Meredith Webber
THE RESCUE DOCTOR'S BABY MIRACLE	
	Dianne Drake
EMERGENCY AT RIVERSIDE HOSPITAL	Joanna Neil

December

SINGLE FATHER, WIFE NEEDED	Sarah Morgan
THE ITALIAN DOCTOR'S PERFECT FAMILY	Alison Roberts
A BABY OF THEIR OWN	Gill Sanderson
THE SURGEON AND THE SINGLE MUM	Lucy Clark
HIS VERY SPECIAL NURSE	Margaret McDonagh
THE SURGEON'S LONGED-FOR BRIDE	Emily Forbes

January

SINGLE DAD, OUTBACK WIFE	Amy Andrews
A WEDDING IN THE VILLAGE	Abigail Gordon
IN HIS ANGEL'S ARMS	Lynne Marshall
THE FRENCH DOCTOR'S MIDWIFE BRIDE	Fiona Lowe
A FATHER FOR HER SON	Rebecca Lang
THE SURGEON'S MARRIAGE PROPOSAL	Molly Evans

MILLS & BOON®

0707 LP 2P P2 Medical